Gentleman
of the Road:

A Hitchhiking Memoir of the 1970s

Between the Lines Publishing
1769 Lexington Ave N, Ste 286
Roseville MN 55108
btwnthelines.com

First Published: October 2023

ISBN: (Paperback) 978-1-958901-48-9
ISBN: (Ebook) 978-1-958901-49-6

Library of Congress Control Number: 2023940499

Gentleman

of the Road:

A Hitchhiking Memoir of the 1970s

Rollie Erickson

"Life is an experimental journey undertaken involuntarily."

—Fernando Pessoa

The Searcher

It was spring in Davenport, Iowa, in the early 1960s when an elderly man stepped out from his porch and filled his lungs with the scent of lilacs growing along the side of his house. The sun was bright, the sky was clear, and the air held a hint of winter's sharpness in its breeze. Across the street was the eight-year-old boy he taught to ride a bike just a short year ago. The boy was sitting on the edge of his terraced lawn like he always did on nice days, watching the world go by. His mother was a young divorcee who had recently remarried and her husband would now take on those fatherly duties of showing the child how to fish, how to hunt, and how to throw a football.

The man sat down on his steps and waved to the boy who waved back. Suddenly, the young stepfather strode directly from the front door of the little gray house, yanked the kid to his feet and dragged him swiftly in, yelling, "I told you not to sit on that grass!"

It was a little disturbing, but not uncommon, to witness such family theater in this neighborhood of modest houses that sat upon terraces, facing the trough of the street. But once the exeunt was performed, and the actors had left the stage, there wasn't much left to think other than, "Wonder what the kid did? He always sits there on sunny days."

What the neighbor never saw was the beating that took place inside the house—how the boy was dragged past his mother whose meaningless look of concern would not alter his fate; how the stepfather had slipped off his belt and barked orders for the boy to pull down his pants; how the executioner proceeded to administer corporal punishment to that bare rump, incising it with bloodied welts; how the tears and snot gushed into one humiliated pool upon the killing floor. And the reason for this punishment? For disobeying orders to not sit on the newly seeded grass on an area of lawn that was worn down by the kid who always sat there—his favorite place. That boy was me.

Mom divorced when I was three years old. I didn't remember a lot about my biological father or the divorce, other than I was living in a desert one day, and moving into a tiny, gray-shingled house the next. The Midwestern sun was weaker and friendlier than the incessant rays that ruled the desert. I didn't know what was going on, or why I was in this new place. I was too young to miss my father or think much about him, but I did remember the deep red rust of the landscape I had left. I remembered Moab, Utah.

I also remembered a lot of traveling, mostly at night. I grew accustomed to the bluish lights of the bus terminal and the soft sickly fragrance of the air-conditioned breeze wafting up from tiny holes at the window. There was something so unreal about it all; a nocturnal adventure that seemed to have no end. I had a stuffed animal that I always brought with me. It shared my shallow sleep as I curled into a second-class seat on a train stretching far and away into a black eternity. Moonlight glided over sleeping faces.

After the move there were not many men in our lives other than my grandfather and an occasional visit from my uncle, my mother's brother. It was just me, Mom, Grandma, and my great-grandmother. My mother was good to me then; she was just a regular Mom and we got along fine. She was also a devout Catholic and took me to church every Sunday, explaining carefully how God sees everything and takes care of us all. But I could tell on occasion that she was troubled. It's not easy being a single parent. Sometimes she would ask me if I thought she was mean or a bad mother. I was dumbfounded. I didn't know what she was talking about. She said that Great-grandma, the kindly old lady that I knew, was a much different person when my mother was a child. My great-grandmother took care of her while her mother, my grandmother, was at work and she was apparently quite mean to Mom. She told her that she, "didn't like little girls," and would chase her around the house, swatting at her with a broom while Mom cowered under a bed. I was only five or six years old when she told me this and it worried me; something was not right. Was Great-grandma troubled as a child too? And was she passing that on to my mother? Would I inherit my mother's problems? I would try to be a comfort to her and be the "little man" of the house. She was often depressed and lonely.

Mom had to work and that meant leaving me with a neighbor who babysat kids all day, one family at a time. We called her "Grandma-Next-Door." She didn't want me to play with other kids for fear of my getting hurt and then not getting paid. But being left behind like this, unable to be with my mother and not allowed to play with other kids, fostered feelings of loneliness and anguish. I remember looking at the torn cellophane on a box of cough drops my mother had given me for the day and worrying that the wrapper could not be restored to its pristine condition—that there was no going back. It made me very sad. Everything was moving irrevocably into the future and leaving an irretrievable past. I had an epiphany in the garden, under a plum tree with its white blossoms and black branches blowing in the wind: a moment of clarity where I was absolutely alone in the world.

We also lived next to a boarding house that was run by a fat older woman, Mrs. Nouse. She had dark circles under her bulging eyes that always reminded me of Black Moors, a type of black goldfish I had seen at the local Woolworth's. Mrs. Nouse's boarding house was a temporary home for out-of-town businessmen and other drifters who came and went on a weekly basis. She was gossipy and a snoop but had a big heart. She felt sorry for my mother and me living alone and would offer to bring us some of her homemade pies. The smell of fried chicken hung about her kitchen window and slipped over the hedge that separated our houses. Sometimes we would be invited over for a game of Chinese checkers with her guests in the evenings. These were warm summer nights on her porch, the players bathed in a drowsy yellow light bombarded by moths. And this is where my mother met Elroy, a young insurance adjuster new in town.

Elroy was a jovial young man who enjoyed good company and a game of cards. With his pale blue eyes, wavy thinning hair and stocky figure he made quite an impression on my mother. "He looks just like Bing Crosby," she would say. "And he's not fat, he's barrel-chested." Elroy was quite taken by my mother's beauty as well, and he made a calculated effort to be kind to me. On these sociable sultry nights, he would take me in his car to a Dairy Queen and buy cones for everyone. We'd bring the treats back to the game, melting ice cream running stickily over my fingers and the cardboard tray.

One day I was out in the yard when I noticed that Elroy was on top of our roof. He had propped up a ladder and was in the process of carrying up swathes of shingles to repair it. A thought came to me so strongly it was as if someone were speaking directly into my ear. The message was an absurd impossibility, a *what if* or *wouldn't it be funny if*, and the blank to be filled was, *if he married my mom*. Strong premonitions have always come to me in this way, where you can't believe something so silly could actually happen—and as it turns out, it usually does. I soon found out that this would be the case.

And so, Alberta and Elroy were married. I was seven years old at the time and adoption by my new stepfather was also in the bargain. The deal was that, by agreeing to be adopted, my biological father would no longer have visiting rights—not that I had seen him in those last four years anyway. There was even a new birth certificate drawn up showing Elroy to be my father. I now had two birth certificates: a real one naming George Grandbouche as my father and the other naming Elroy, the adoptive fake. I was now George Rollie Erickson.

Unfortunately, George would also have to sign off on this arrangement. I don't know why he did. He had always sent me wonderful gifts and expensive toys: a Lionel train, fancy dump trucks, and a big metal airplane with folding wings. She let me keep most of them but after a while some of these toys would mysteriously disappear.

"Oh, we can't keep these," my mother would say, or "He's not your real father anymore and he doesn't really love you." She told me that Elroy was to be my *real* father now and that he loved me. Funny I never actually heard Elroy say that he loved me, or ever say he was sorry about anything. I guess that made me his *real* child. This pantomime was strictly for the benefit of my mother who needed the fantasy of a happy family.

"He's a man, he doesn't know how to express affection very well," my mother would say. As far as I was concerned, he loved me like a farmer loves his animals, taking care of them so that they may be presentable when brought to market. And Elroy's side of the family was so foreign to me. They were lethally serious Evangelical Lutherans from the dark

6

hinterlands of northern Minnesota—a veritable breeding ground for Christian World Domination.

A year or two into the marriage things changed dramatically. Elroy was no longer the kind man I had met playing Chinese checkers and buying everyone ice cream. Having him as my new real father took some getting used to but I gave it my best shot. Every kid has a dad, don't they? I wanted one too but what I got was something less benign. Criticism became paramount to his style of parenting, and I was continually yelled at. He was also quite taciturn; it was as if you were supposed to read his mind, or rather, you shouldn't have to read his mind because everything he said and did was self-explanatory for anyone with a brain. On weekends Elroy sat in the living room, in his favorite chair, and puffed away on his pipe, listening to a ballgame on the radio while simultaneously watching a different game on television. A sea of smoke filled the room and hung there— you could swim through it. Perhaps his thoughts were being expressed in smoke signals. At other times, when I was engaged in something creative like drawing or painting, or building a model car, he would say, "you copied that," or "the wheels don't turn."

"Your father just tells it like it is." my mother would say to me whenever I complained about him. He was her guiding light, her benefactor, her keeper. In a lot of ways, she was a child herself.

After that initial beating my mother told him never to do it again, and he didn't. But he probably convinced her that, if

7

that's the case, then she had better start disciplining me herself. I could hear them having lengthy discussions in the living room about me as I was trying to go to sleep (this would continue into my teens). And so began the beatings from my mother who, until then, had never resorted to such behavior. This was a game changer for me. I felt betrayed. I started stuttering and had to get control of myself to stop it. I was beaten for the least infraction and started having nightmares of abandonment. Meanwhile my mother, in some preposterous way, had become a black hole for the garnering of sympathy from all our relatives; poor "Bert," she has so many problems.

Even though my mother was now the executioner, I still had to align myself with her for fear of dealing with Elroy. She was a known, he was an unknown. Now, after a beating, I would go into my room and spit on the rosary that hung on my bedpost. God was of no recourse. And I was never able to fully articulate this betrayal to my mother; she wouldn't have understood anyway. All I knew was that I felt abandoned at a gut level.

The irony is that, before their marriage, I was a very well-behaved and sensitive kid. I didn't require discipline for the purpose of increasing my intelligence. I was already smart enough to know that Elroy was an outsider, a foreign usurper of power, goose-stepping into the kingdom of my home. Elroy would eventually insinuate his place in this family, but the invasion created damage, and it was something I had to stuff. I will say this though: he was certainly very good at demanding fear and respect, which appeared to be the only goal. From Elroy's point of view, I'm sure he felt he was doing the right thing. And, lacking experience, what else is a twenty-seven-year-old man going to come up with for raising a seven-year-old kid from another marriage? He just didn't know any better. To him, this was how you raised a child because this was how he was raised. He grew up on a farm where hard work replaced creative outlets, and hard lessons replaced praise. He was always admonishing himself for not doing something right: a beautiful coffee table that he built in his shop would, according to him, have numerous defects; he would never accept simple praise. Moreover, he never spoke well of his own father who was an alcoholic that abused him and his mother. In fact, he never spoke of his father ever, even if you asked about him; he would just shrug and mumble something inconsequential, something of no interest. Likewise, he had a brother but never spoke of him either, only that he too was an alcoholic who ran away from home. Elroy was the mystery man; family stories were not forthcoming.

When I was nine, I wanted to run away but didn't have the nerve. One night I thought I would take off for my grandmother's house in Rock Island. I even had a map of the city streets and tried to imagine how long it would take to get there. My cousin Bobby was staying overnight and, while we were getting into our pajamas, I showed him the city map I had stuffed under the bed.

"Look what I've got."

"What is it?"

"It's a map of Davenport and Rock Island. Here's where we are." I pointed to a little square on the hand-drawn map. "And here's where Grandma lives."

"Yeah? So what?"

"So, I'm going to use it to run away. I'm going to go live with Grandma. I can't stand living here anymore."

Bobby just laughed. "You won't do it."

"You bet I will. I'm leaving tonight at midnight. I'm going right out that window."

"I'll bet you don't. I'll bet you're here in the morning."

"You'll see…I'll be gone at midnight…if I wake up."

I didn't wake up. Looking at the route now I can see that it was an impossible four or five miles of city streets. I was more afraid of Elroy than I was of getting picked up by the cops. I realized I would have to ingratiate myself to their absurdities in order to survive. I would even have to be sympathetic, instinctually shifting into a classic Stockholm syndrome.

Because of the trust that was lost, I would not be taking any advice from them no matter how sensible it may have been. I would keep my own council and find things out for myself. I became a searcher. Consequently, my parents' values had lost all meaning to me. That is to say, all things life had to offer had equal weight. There was no greater value placed on the ties of family, or having children, or owning property, or having a good job, or marriage, or money, than there was on anything else. The value of these things would be questioned and personally tested. I was unmoored and sent adrift to see if the world was really flat or round. Even the word "love" became suspect; I had no idea what it meant. My examples of love appeared to be only a routine that people went through propelled by blind assumptions. Since I couldn't get through to my mother that I didn't feel loved by them (such a declaration would, ironically, result in punishment), I turned to others in expression of my grief, only to be told, "Don't be silly, of course your parents love you." It took me a long time to reach the conclusion that maybe everyone was right, that they did love me, it just wasn't something that was of any use to me. I couldn't wait to grow up and get the hell out. More than anything I just wanted my freedom, to run away and never look back.

I told my grandfather when I was eight or nine that I wished I was an adult so nobody could control me anymore. He looked at me sadly and said, "But these are your golden years."

Of course, nothing is total doom and gloom in this life. I was fed, clothed, and sheltered. My grandmother would always defend me. Moreover, there would be birthday parties, holidays and extended family picnics. My mother would give me praise for something I accomplished now and then—Elroy never. To the outside world my parents were Mr. and Mrs. Wonderful and life just went on as if nothing was wrong. And, as in any family, there were plenty of moments of kindness. Elroy did his duty with fatherly advice and even tried his hand at bonding: baseball games, fishing, hunting, etc. And we had a good time doing them. Hunting and walking the land, instilled in me an early love for the poetry of Frost and Sandburg. Very few can say they had a perfect family, and my parents did the best they could with what they had.

If there was one thing my mother had taught me, however, it was that it's okay to "leave the playground." I believe those early trips out of Moab had a deep effect, grounding me to the ever-present possibility of an open door. As much as my mother adopted Elroy's tactics of control in parenting, she also left open a few cracks of leniency through which I could imagine my escape. My mother was a very complicated woman. Despite her need to control, and to be controlled, she could suddenly become quite impulsive with a crazy sort of energy. Like many women in the 60s she relinquished her power to her husband. She was happy to be a housewife and leave the job market when she married Elroy. She had a need for freedom but didn't know how to go about it in a man's world. I could sense there was always trouble brewing beneath the mask of her societal role and these subconscious frustrations would occasionally erupt. I think the fact that she was an amateur artist somehow loosened things up a bit. She was smart enough to allow for an imagination.

My grandmother and my uncle were also artists. Making art was a habit and a natural engagement for this family circle. Mom taught me how to paint with oils when I was very young and my grandmother would take me along on bus trips with her art group to the Art Institute of Chicago (AIC) when I was ten years old. It was the first time I'd ever seen a large museum. The disturbing image of Salvador Dali's flaming giraffes sparked in me a lifelong fascination with Surrealism. I was also quite amazed at seeing the Picassos. Cubism kindled a feeling of familiarity to such an extent that whenever I went to the museum, and saw a Picasso, I felt as if I "owned" it; it belonged to me as I belonged to it. Later I would learn that the AIC has the finest Surrealist collection in the United States and Chicago is home to a group of people who adhere to its tenets both aesthetically and politically (Franklin and Penelope Rosemont, et al). I saw that the imaginative life was the only thing worth pursuing and that art would be the wind in my creative sails, whatever form that would take. The lesson of freedom was this: that no one is free in this life; birds fight over crumbs of bread and even the king and queen of England have to go to work. But in the studio, or whatever creative space you carve out for yourself, you'll find freedom can be negotiated...if not achieved.

Test Run

I first met Jewell when I was a senior in high school, in the small town of Forest Lake, Minnesota. My family moved there when I was in eighth grade. She wasn't part of my gang of friends, my clique. Her group was the jocks, the girlfriends of jocks, and the squeaky-clean church goers. My friends were the hippies, the musicians, the arty types; Jewell's were all the good boys and girls that conservative parents love to see, marching into the future with the banner of the status quo. But Jewell was different. She was a liberal and might even be said to border on the radical. But a lot of us bordered on the radical, given the times and what was going on in Vietnam. She sat behind me in our political science class and was the only one, besides our teacher, with whom I could have an intellectual discussion on almost anything, even politics. Jewel was a brunette with brown eyes and had an inquisitive face anchored by a wry smile; she made a very convincing double for Vermeer's *Girl with a Pearl Earring*. One day I turned to her and said, "I had a dream about you last night. I dreamed we were sitting on the ground at a rock concert, and you shared your blanket with me." I really did have the dream, but I also thought it was a great pick-up line.

"Oh, really?" she said. "Better be careful what you dream."

Sam, another good friend, was a very worldly and soulful cat. He wore John Lennon wire rims and had a haystack head of golden hair. Sam was the one who introduced me to Kerouac's *On the Road* and *The Dharma Bums*, two books that romanticized hitchhiking and the freedom of movement with a searcher starring as the protagonist. Sam was a cross between the two characters in *On the Road*; not as crazy as Dean Moriarty, not as reasonable as Sal Paradise. He also turned me on to Zap Comix and R. Crumb. I used to kid him that he was Mr. Natural while I was Flakey Foont. We shared an interest in Buddhism and Sam started practicing Transcendental Meditation. We also liked reading Abbie Hoffman's *Steal this Book* (my shoplifting trophy). He and his brother took the dreaded LSD and went on road trips together out West— coming back with all sorts of lovely lurid tales. There was something mystical about Sam, and like me, he was a searcher. And like Sal Paradise he had a ne'er-do-well's reputation with the small-town cops who were always stopping him for no good reason, presumably to find some illegal substance on his poor, misunderstood, person. Sam turned me on to hashish on my seventeenth birthday.

I was becoming more independent, much to my mother's consternation. Whenever I asserted myself, she would say, "You're acting just like George!" This was meant as a reproach, but it had the opposite effect. I started thinking that maybe this George guy was alright after all. An outburst like that from her was also rather curious because it was taboo to talk of him. When we lived in Davenport, before Elroy came along, she stored boxes of photos that were filled with images of George on the top shelf of my bedroom closet. She took the trouble to point them out and told me never to go up there because it contained pictures of *him*. I had no desire, and even if I did, I was too small then to even reach it. I wondered why she kept them there or why she bothered to tell me of the contents. But now, as I was coming of age, she pulled out all these photographs from her cedar chest and showed them to me. I guess she must have thought enough time had passed that I wouldn't get any reckless ideas of looking him up. This private showing was prefaced with, "You look so much like George."

The box contained pictures of a silver trailer parked in the desert; the happy young couple holding their newborn; my skinny father in baggy flags of pants and my mother in curvaceous jeans with her wild Irish hair, freckles, and a small space between her front teeth. Images caught in the light of a bygone era yet seemingly as fresh as yesterday.

"Where were these taken?" I asked.

"I don't know, somewhere out in the desert. Your biological father was a geologist. He worked for the government, prospecting for uranium."

16

"Well, that must have been…exciting, no?"

"I hated it out there, out in the middle of nowhere. And you didn't know who or what was going to happen next. I was riding in a jeep once with a prospector friend of his and we stopped to help a stranger on the road. George's friend reached for a gun under the seat and kept his hand on it while he talked to the guy…you just never knew."

"Scary," I said.

"And there were always these poor filthy Indians hanging around. It was horrible. We finally got a house in Moab; that was a little better."

I winced at the "filthy Indians" comment and changed the subject. "Believe it or not, I do remember the house…and even snatches of that trailer."

"You do? You know, there was a rattlesnake under the steps of the trailer door that your father, I mean George, had to remove."

"So it was all horrible? What did you do for fun?" I asked.

"Oh, there were some grand parties. It was hard to get alcohol in Utah so the only place where the liquor would flow was at somebody's house. And there were some Westerns being made out there so wealthy folks in town would put on a party for these Hollywood actors. I met Dana Andrews…he picked you up and held you in the air.

"Oh…that's cool." I didn't know who Dana Andrews was.

"He was a famous actor," my mother said, as if reading my mind.

17

She dug to the bottom of the box and pulled out their old wedding picture, now faded into a rosy patina. The groom had sparkling black eyes, a rather pronounced uni-brow, and was wearing a grin as wide as his future. Hanging on his arm was a strangely blank woman with pale blue eyes and a quasi-smile as enigmatic and detached as the Mona Lisa. It looked wrong, where was the happiness? I asked her what she was feeling that day but all I got was a disingenuous and totally forgettable answer. Perhaps she had her doubts.

"What happened, Mom? Why did you get divorced?" I asked.

"Oh, he was a flirt, a real womanizer. He didn't really love me. He deserted me," she said.

"Really? Aw, I'm sorry...that's not right," I said.

"And he took me away from my religion."

"Oh," I didn't know what else to say to that. How do you take someone away from their religion? You either have it or you don't.

"But your father loves me and that's all that matters."

By "father" she meant Elroy of course. I could tell, even as a teenager, that my mother in her simplicity had a lot more going on than met the eye. There were some complexities here that I wasn't sure I wanted to pursue any further.

"And I have you. You'll always be my little baby no matter how old you get."

"Oh...yeah...great," I half smiled.

Gentleman of the Road

Other than Jim Morrison, Janice Joplin and Jimi Hendrix all perishing within months of each other, my senior year of high school was very enjoyable—mostly because I could see it all coming to an end. I had a car, a part time job, some friends, and even a date or two. Jewell and I didn't formally date so much as we just enjoyed hanging out together. I'd even bring Sam along sometimes, but I had to leave him at the corner, pick her up, and then drive back to get him. Sam had a reputation. Jewell's father didn't like him, and by association, didn't like me.

I worked at a restaurant in town called Der Lak Haus. It was the fancy place you took your date to when you wanted to impress her on a Saturday night. The head chef, Oscar, was very sensitive. If a patron sent their steak back because it was too rare, he would return it burnt to a crisp. Once he got so mad, he picked up a cleaver and pitched it, professional baseball style, into the wooden door going to the basement—just before a busboy was headed up the stairs and into the kitchen. He took one look at the door's new addition and resigned on the spot.

The restaurant is long gone now—burned to the ground. Perhaps Oscar went too far in charring someone's steak. It was the location, however, of my first art sale. The owner liked a painting of mine and let me hang it in the bar. I really admired Andrew Wyeth at the time (still do) and did a watercolor of a big field and hill with a weathered house perched at the top. I painted every blade of grass. It was called "The Spring's Place," which was a deserted farmhouse belonging to a family

19

named Spring where Elroy and I used to hunt. I also wrote a poem about it, having just discovered poetry, emulating Sandburg or Frost. The painting sold for sixty dollars—a tidy sum for a seventeen-year-old in 1970.

After high school I thought it was time to have a little adventure before starting out for college. I planned a tour around the state, and north into Canada, with my 1963 Dodge Dart. I figured it would take about a week. Sam would come with me on this odyssey, but of course, I couldn't let my parents know that. I don't know how they caught wind of his reputation! It's not like we had any social connections living out in the rural area of Lino Lakes. My parents had no friends or social interactions with anyone other than relatives. I took the old slow road, a veritable patchwork of asphalt that connects to Forest Lake where Sam lived. Interstate 35 was fairly new and the branch that was near my house was nothing more than a runway of compacted dirt. I had a friend who lived next to it. He had a green souped-up '57 Chevy that he was forever working on right in the middle of what would become 35W. He'd ask if I'd like to take a test run and we would drag down that naked stretch doing a hundred mph, clouds of dust pluming like a grassfire. The engine was so large it made the car twitch from side to side when he shifted gears. But now I was late, and it was mid-morning by the time I got to Sam's. I knocked on his door and his mom answered.

"Sorry I'm kinda late," I said. "Is Sam ready?"

"Ready for what?" she said.

"We're…going…on a trip," I faltered.

"Oh, I don't know. He's upstairs, asleep."

I couldn't believe this guy. He didn't tell anyone he'd be gone for a week? I burst into his tiny room, not much bigger than his Dylan poster.

"What the hell? Get up, you're wasting our time!"

"Oh man, I'm hungover. I need a cigarette." Sam's household, like most of my friends, permitted chaos. I was envious.

After breakfast and several cups of coffee, it was afternoon when we finally threw his crap into the car and headed north. We made good time on the interstate until the outskirts of Duluth and then had to pick our way through town. In Duluth we caught Highway 53 and headed for International Falls. I could feel the emotional weight of my parents lifting as we climbed out of the hills and looked back at the great expanse of the inland sea, Lake Superior. I hadn't felt so happy and exhilarated in a long time. Other than those somnambulist trips my mother and I took out of Moab, the only other time I felt this excited was when I struck out on my own a few years ago when I took a train to visit my grandmother in Rock Island. It was one of the last runs of the Rock Island Line in the late 1960s. I walked through coaches that were very nearly empty, a ghost town on wheels, and found a seat in the luxury section. No one cared where you sat. The seats were huge and cushiony and could swivel. There were very few of them and you had a lot of space. I sat down in front of a picture window and just watched the spring greening of the countryside go whizzing by while the car

21

bounced with a lazy rebound, making you feel like you were in a boat or an old Cadillac with bad shocks. Wanderlust was pretty strong in me then. I just wanted to ride the rails and be free like a hobo. And now, at last, I was on the road again.

We almost made it to Canada that day, but the waning light bade us find something quick that looked like supper and a campsite. We picked up some hotdogs, bread, and cans of beans and set up camp in the twilight. I brought out my twenty-dollar Sears guitar and faked some blues using an old copper pipe for a slide. It was Kumbaya time around the fire. Sam was impressed. The pipe chewed up the strings. Mosquitos ate us alive that night in the floorless and screen-less canvas pup tent I brought, so we slept in the car for the rest of the trip.

The next day we picked up two hitchhikers, a girl and a guy, a little older than us. Sam and I were keen on going to Canada because rumor had it that the beer was of a higher octane. This was in the days of Schlitz, Blatz, Falstaff, and my favorite, Grain Belt—all with a low ABV. The four of us crossed over into Fort Frances, meandered west, and caught the Trans-Canada Highway going north. Somewhere along the way, near Lake of the Woods, we stopped and set up camp. I bought a couple of six packs. I don't think the beer was any better, but it got us where we wanted to be, one step removed and free as a bird. The hitchhikers had set up their tent and were inside, going at it hot and heavy. They were quite noisy and entertaining. Sam was an interested voyeur, but it was all a mystery to me that had yet to be unveiled. I left them their privacy.

In the morning we left the hitchhikers and drove further north, taking the Trans-Canada going west. It was also called the "Kings Highway." Sam noticed we were riding the King's Highway going west, just like the Door's song, "The End." We rambled through Winnipeg for no good reason other than to say we went there, and afterwards, promptly headed south through enormous fields of sunflowers. At some point I decided to part my hair in the middle and let it grow long. My parents were always making me get a haircut, but the evaporation of their jurisdiction was palpable now and it didn't seem to matter anymore. Nothing mattered; I was free. I took a knife and carved off a hunk to even it out while sitting around the campfire. I also purchased a pair of wire rims at an antique store that resembled Ray Manzarek's, the keyboard player for the Doors. I'd have my lenses fit when I got back.

We flowed south into the Dakotas on a lazy road that runs parallel to an old railroad track for much of the border with Minnesota. All the small towns along the way looked the same: a grain elevator near the tracks, a few small buildings, a house, a bar, a church, and then…repeat.

Sam settled back, stuck his bare foot out the window and lit up a cigarette. "Man, usually when I go on the road there's always something to learn, you know? There's always a cosmic truth. Like when that guy in *The Dharma Bums* is running so fast down a steep hill on a mountain and he says, 'You can't fall off a mountain.' Whenever my brother and I went on the road there was some cosmic truth to be learned. But I ain't seen nuthin' on this trip."

"Maybe you were on acid then," I said. I felt bad. Sam was right, there wasn't a lot of cosmic truth happening being wrapped up in the luxury of a four wheeled tin box. Maybe hitching would have pulled the cosmic switch? I was just happy to be away from my parents and even happier contemplating the coming fall when I would be off to school in Duluth; far enough away from them to start my own life. I would leave home at eighteen and never go back.

Jewell told me before I left that she and her friend Dawn would be camping at such-and-so park by the end of the week and would I like to stop and visit before heading back into the Twin Cities? I told Sam to pull out the map and plot a course. "What? Jewelly and Dawny? Damn, you didn't tell me there'd be wimmin!" We pulled into their camp in the late afternoon, pooled our resources for a supper and stayed the night. We were all having a great time, happy to be done with high school and looking forward to our newly found independence. Dawn was a pretty Minnesota blonde with an open smile and a gentle personality. She had a contrapuntal energy and countenance to Jewell's swarthiness and abruptness. Jewell was brusque yet affable. A common ground in their friendship was a sardonic sense of humor that always sparked when they were together and could be quite infectious. Jewell was especially good at it. Once, when we were walking past a porn shop and theater that advertised "Girls! Girls! Girls!" she performed cartwheels, as a joke, in front of the place.

They invited us into their tent for the night, which was awfully nice since we were pretty tired of curling up on car seats. Later, Jewell and I shared some intimacy as discreetly as possible with two other sleepers nearby. Of course, we didn't get away with it—both of them spying on us just as discreetly.

"Boy, ain't you the ladies' man!" Sam guffawed as we pulled out of camp the next morning.

"Uhm ... I take it you were awake."

"Oh yeah, Dawn was too. Hyaw, hyaw, hyaw, yer a regular pimp!" Sam liked being obnoxious. He had a twinkle in his eye...and so did I. After an hour the Twin Cities skyline rose in the east. Van "The Man" Morrison's new album, *Moondance*, came on the radio and we were sailing "Into the Mystic."

When I dropped him at his door, Sam said, "You know, I said there wasn't anything cosmic to learn on this trip but I was wrong. There's always something to learn. The road always teaches you something."

He never explained what it was he learned. I suppose cosmic truths are ineffable. But I certainly had a bounce in my step when I got home. I'm sure Mom and Elroy were wondering what was with the central parting of my short hair, with one side sticking out, making me look as disheveled as Rimbaud. And like the poet, I had acquired a deep desire to ramble. Who knows? Maybe next time I'd ditch the car, stick my thumb out, and ride the wind to wherever it takes me.

The summer was coming to an end and it was time to say goodbye to my small town. None of my closer friends would go on to college. I don't know what became of them. Mindsets change when faced with the reality of moving on and making a living. It was not possible to keep friendships going for longer than a year after that. Reality would be deferred for me (in more ways than one) over the next four years. Sam and I parted on a sour note. I don't know why or whatever became of him. Of course, the jocks and "churchies" (virtually the same people) were financially better off than most and would go either to the University of Minnesota Minneapolis, or Duluth campus. Jewell went to Minneapolis, and our friendship ended, but not because of our parting for separate schools. It ended because her father forbade her to see me anymore. I thought this rather strange since we were both free now and able to choose our own friends. I especially thought it strange since Jewell was such a feminist and ought to be expressing her basic rights. I guess father-daughter relationships go deep. She had lots of tears, and I just can't, and blah blah blah. It was just as well. And, anyway, it would only be the first time we'd leave each other on our see-saw ride of abandonments.

Duluth

Duluth was a funky old town back in the day. And it still is. The city fathers have done their dutiful best to give the place a facelift for those tourist dollars, but its backbone is just as raw and decayed as it ever was. It's the citadel by an unforgiving sea, the last ragged ramparts against serious oblivion. And I love it that way. Nature is always an integral part of this cityscape. You don't need to go far to be in the woods. There are even stories of bears wandering into town, following mailmen.

The University of Minnesota, Duluth (UMD) is situated at the top of the hill, and like a lot of universities, it has a sculpture by Jacques Lipchitz (think *Song of the Vowels*, ad infinitum). UMD, however, has *Sieur DuLut* depicting Daniel Greysolon, Sieur du Lhut, the French explorer and Duluth's namesake pointing towards Lake Superior. It looks like a pile of cow dung with one arm doing a hip-shot and the other holding forth a hotdog. The feeling amongst art students was that maybe Lipchitz did it as a joke. The sculptor is best as a cubist, yet some of his work has this billowing cartoonish Mannerism of late Renaissance flair and *Sieur DuLut* is one of them. And so there I was in a beginning drawing class, sketching this sculpture in the little cul-de-sac on campus where it lives.

One of my favorite teachers at Duluth was Phil Meany. There was something, an aura, about him that I noticed right away before ever talking to him. He always seemed to be beaming as he moved down the halls with a purposeful swiftness of step. A quick intelligence lived behind those blue eyes and closely trimmed gray beard. Phil turned me on to conceptual art and the idea that art was a process, not a means to an end. He taught printmaking, drawing, and the philosophy of art. Although I was a painter, mired in the millennia old aesthetics where painting lives, I wanted to create something that questioned the nature of art and painting in particular. The invitation to throw away the paintbrush and engage in the cerebral games of conceptual art appealed to me at the time. Phil provided support for that. In a way, he was a father figure to me although I don't think he knew that, nor do I think he would have approved of such sentimentality. But I trusted his judgment and the impartiality he gave in the presentation of various ideas and aesthetics. He was the most well-balanced person I have ever met.

Jewell had come up at the beginning of freshman year to see some of her friends and tried to revive our friendship. But

I gave her the cold shoulder and sent her off crying. It was a hard thing to do, but really, time to move on. Who wants to be bogged down with a high school romance?

Freshman year, unfortunately, became an academic disaster for me. Duluth was a party school, and I was still partying like a high schooler. It didn't help that the most boring classes were the first ones required. Elroy had provided a scholarship for me through his employer, but to keep it I had to maintain a B average or better. My first quarter yielded a C average and so my scholarship was lost for that year. Even if I had brought it up the next quarter to an A level it would be a no go. I had to wait until the end of the next school year to prove myself. Elroy was furious that he'd have to pay for all of next year. If it hadn't been for a thing called Freshman Studies, an experimental program that was run by a couple of philosophy professors, it would have been the end of my academic life. Some of the academic requirements for freshman year were lifted via this experimental course. As an art major, I was free to create something on my own and present it to the class. I made a couple of avant-garde films featuring the music of Oscar Peterson in one and Captain Beefheart in another. Ray, my new acquaintance in the class, donated the Oscar Peterson. Ray was a tall drink of water with scraggly thinning hair that made him look like a well-used paint brush. I told him I needed a jazz piece that was three minutes long, for the purpose of time-fitting a typical 8mm spool of film. We went to his dorm room and rifled through his four-foot-long stack of records piled up against the wall;

here was everything you'd ever want if you were stuck on a desert island. He pulled out the album—the song was *Jim*, clocking in at 3:04. The teachers, being beatniks from another era, really dug it. I passed, and Ray and I became fast friends.

I was very depressed at having lost the scholarship and was practically suicidal. Of course, feeling suicidal and actually doing it are two different things—I could never understand suicide as a remedy since you wouldn't be around to profit from it. More than anything, I was simply afraid of having to return home in this defeated state. I couldn't even stand the thought of going home for holidays, and very often made excuses not to; I relished my freedom. I told Ray all this. He looked at me and said, "Let's do some acid." Being so low I just thought, why not? Here was an opportunity to step outside myself. I decided it best to just shift some gears and jump off the scaffolding of reason like the island men of Vanuatu (from whence we get bungee jumping—not a thing in 1971!).

We crushed some Orange Barrel and snorted it so the effect would be fairly quick, and the trip wouldn't last as long. After that we marched over to the cafeteria before it closed for supper. I was dawdling with my scalloped potatoes, noticing how strangely people were moving, how they seemed to be leaving traces of themselves behind like a soft strobe light; motion was arrested and displayed in a viscous chunk of space and time. Students were milling about, looking like Hindu gods with multiple appendages. I was seeing "tracers." I was also becoming quite gleeful. Ray seemed a bit perturbed and

30

said, "Uh ... I'll meet you downstairs in the student lounge." I poked at my potatoes and marveled at how industrial they looked. The server at the food line had slapped the potatoes on my plate in such a way as to leave an ejecta blanket, like you see around moon craters, affecting certain areas of my chipped beef landscape. The more I thought about it, the more everything became mechanical looking: the stainless-steel tubs of food, the metal tables, plastic chairs, and fiberglass trays. Here we all were, in a line, unconscious of the machinery that seemed to be the dominating force of which we were an integral part. The machine would ultimately be pumping us out into society, and this was its nursery. I became un-hungry. I started to worry about Ray and decided to go find him. Who the hell knows if he would really be in the lounge or even how long ago it was he said he was going there. Time? What is time? I looked at my watch and thought how ridiculous it was to be handcuffed to this mechanical device. So I went to find him and there he was, sitting in a chair, seemingly reading a newspaper. And he would have looked normal too...if he didn't have the newspaper upside down! I guess the universe gave him a 50/50 chance at subterfuge, but he had missed one tiny detail. We wandered around the campus and then took refuge in Ray's room. To celebrate our enhanced state of mind he put on a Jimi Hendrix album, *Electric Ladyland*, where an eerie UFO-sounding track inspired me to envision a mathematical formula for anti-gravity. I actually saw the equation floating in front of me but, like Coleridge's *Kubla Khan*, the vision melted when the track ended. I can't recall what happened the rest of the night except that, at some point, we became madmen racing down campus halls, dissipating some pent-up energy like the eighteen-year-olds that we were.

Ray would become part of a shifting group of fellow trippers, mostly guys. Larry, another group member, was insanely together. I watched him once when we were on acid, flipping a razor blade and catching it in the palm of his hand like someone would play with a coin...without cutting himself. Another time I watched him balance on an icy railing. He was always the tripped-out daredevil, earning him the role of undesignated driver. I say undesignated because he was tripping like the rest of us! He'd taxi us around, a bunch of freaks in highly suggestable LSD mode, and say, "Hey, if I run this old lady down, I could put another notch on the side of my car." We'd titter nervously. But I always put my intrinsic trust in him; I knew that he knew what he was doing.

As strange as some of these experiences were, they didn't seem any different than a dream. We see unexplainable stuff in our dreams all the time and yet somehow, they become acceptable because that part of us becomes the *other*, the *observer*. I never had a bad trip, but I knew others who had. Psychedelics simply remove the boundaries between dreaming and waking life while slowing you down, so you can observe all the incoming data in its raw form. I began to realize that the fixed narratives directing our relationship to the world were just a script we've come to believe as real, or perhaps, what we've agreed to collectively accept as reality. The psychedelic, or magic, world is there all the time. You just have to slow down to see it. I was never much of a meditator, but I was convinced that meditation could produce a similar effect. Acid showed me that life was worth living; it was my DIY shrink. The Surrealists would have loved this stuff.

If the initial betrayal I had felt as a child was the unmooring of my boat from the harbor of "family," the use of psychedelics was the unmooring of my boat from the harbor I called "myself." Who was this Self? Not only was there no longer a hierarchical value placed on things that society had to offer, there was no longer a recognizable value placed on what I called myself. Who was this I? This I was no longer a pronoun—it was a verb, something that moved, something that changed, something that was habitually evolving. These thoughts were strangely freeing and yet confounding. I was still a searcher and a little bit lost.

Acid also showed me that I had to grow up. Consequently, my grades improved. The powers that be, the morons of academia, were not going to let me major in art because I was getting nothing but Cs in my intro to art classes. So I skipped the boring garbage, those preliminary courses, and took any advanced ones open to me. I was then able to maintain a B average and got my scholarship back.

By the end of sophomore year, I had given up mind-altering substances (except for alcohol and pot) and was getting my act together academically. Although my grades had improved, I was still in this fragile state of mind from the drugs. It was in this blurry transitional state that I decided to write Jewell. I'm not sure how or why it was that I happened to have her address. I wrote to other old friends as well, hoping to repair this lost sense of self. As one can imagine, Jewell was quite inhospitable. Still, she was one of the most real people I had at that time to talk to. I was okay with any criticism directed my way since that would help me pick up the pieces and make sense of my life. After a while, the letters became more conciliatory, and a regular correspondence was maintained. Jewell, as it turned out, was also an artist, a writer. She still considered herself a feminist and introduced me to a cadre of women authors. An evolving comradery was taking place as we cast our critical eyes at the world. We decided to meet once again. She was waiting for me, sitting in the sun at the end of a dock that was on a small pond at her parents' house. I was surprised by her embrace. There was something different about it; not just old friends saying hello. There appeared to be a real connection happening and I felt completely at home. I wasn't expecting that. One thing led to another and pretty soon we were a couple again.

Jewell came up to Duluth and went to school with me for the spring quarter of our junior year. That summer we rented a cheap cabin perched on the edge of a cliff that overlooked Lake Superior. Sometimes the wind would blow for days, and I thought the cabin could easily be blown out to sea. At some point, we got the notion to blow out of there ourselves, just like the wind. We would leave the Midwest behind and see what we could make of the world at hand. Jewell and I questioned the validity of this prescribed life that was looming in front of us. One afternoon, while making a pie from the ubiquitous thimbleberries that grew near our cabin (the pie became a watery disaster), Jewell turned to me and said, "Can you believe we only have one year of school left?"

"No, it's unreal. And then what do you do after that?"

"We're supposed to get jobs and become productive members of society."

"Ha! Yeah, somehow, I can't see that. The only thing I can do with an art degree is teach and you need a master's for that. I can't imagine giving up your life for a menial job straight out of college. And then what about us? Get married? Buy a house, and have two point four children?"

Jewell said, "Marriage is an entrapment created by men. You don't need a document that says you're a couple. We just need a vacation. Where would you like to go?"

"I've always wanted to go to California; maybe San Francisco," I said. "What about you?"

"I'd go anywhere. San Francisco sounds great. I'm tired of living in the Midwest."

"Me too. Hey, let's just go. Why get stuck in all this? Let's just hitchhike the hell out of here."

"All the way to California?"

"Why not? We'll be hobos for the summer. If we like it, we'll stay."

"Our parents would freak."

"So what? This is our time. And anyway, we're different, we're artists. We're free."

35

I was mildly fascinated with the hobo thing. The road trip with Sam a few years ago still lingered with me, and I wondered what it would have been like if we had just hitched around the state. What would travel without a safety net show me about the world and how bad could it possibly be? The only hobo I had met was someone Jewell picked up off the street a year earlier when she was living in Minneapolis. Always being the rescuer, she let him stay for one night on the living room floor of the house she shared with her housemate, Rita. He was young with black hair and had the bluest eyes I'd ever seen; eyes that held a strange combination of fear and repose. He was always looking through you, not at you, a haunted young man. He was also quite unwashed with patches of a black patina, no doubt acquired from the grime of a boxcar. He said he was crowned "Prince of the Hobos" down in Iowa. Later I found that to be a lie. There is no crowning of a "Prince." There is, however, a crowning of the "King of the Hobos" held annually at the National Hobo Convention in Britt, Iowa.

But most of our friends would settle for the house, the car, the kids—and why not? Their family ties were more in the "normal" range of the social spectrum. As wide as the generation gap was for everyone back then, they still had enough heartfelt ties. Teach your children well, so the song goes. Jewell had close ties to her family too, but she also had enough of an adventurous spirit to test those ties. We decided to leave Duluth, go to the Minneapolis campus for senior year, and then take off into the great unknown. Having read *On the*

36

Road as a teenager had a lot to do with my romanticizing about life on the road. That notion I had earlier while traveling with Sam of ditching the car and thumbing to Elsewhere was beginning to resemble reality. We would leave in a year, as soon as the snow melted and the sun brought a promise of warmer nights.

On the day that we left the cabin, a huge rainbow formed over Lake Superior—we took it as a good omen. And as poor as I was, I dug into my pocket, took a fistful of change and threw it as hard as I could into the lake screaming, "FUCK MONEY!" I was sick of having to worry all the time about money and my future. I thought of this gesture as an exorcism. The coins are still there.

Moving to the Twin Cities was an eye opener. I could see why Jewell preferred it, although I did miss the natural beauty that envelops Duluth. It was great to see real art for a change at the Walker Art Center and the Minneapolis Institute of Art. The West Bank, near the campus, was the hip place to score pot when I was in high school, and it hadn't changed much in these few years. This was the center of Minneapolis counterculture back in the day. There's an old building on the corner of Cedar and Riverside that once had a kitchen run by your local friendly anarchists. At the time it was called The New Riverside Café. You could get a bowl of chili for whatever price you wanted to pay, and they would give you the same cheery "thank you" no matter if you paid fifty cents or fifty dollars. Their windows displayed the local community news and opinions, written in large white letters, directly on the glass. Stuff like: "RENTERS UNION STRIKE TODAY!" and "STAND UP TO THE FASCIST PIGS!" (or something similar). The anarchists also used a long room for a music hall where I saw an old blues pianist—I can't recall his name. And a young Greg Brown, the renowned poet folk singer from Iowa, giving a free Thanksgiving dinner concert there for all the bums and winos (including us). He stood up there in overalls and sang "Rooty Toot Toot for the Moon." There was also the ubiquitous headshop on the block, and an antique clothing store—supply for all the anti-fashion hippie fashionistas. The Electric Fetus, a great place for records, was right across the street. Willie Murphy and The Bumble Bees (later just "The Bees") played regularly around the corner on Riverside. We bought our camping gear and backpacks for our anticipated trip to the coast at Midwest Mountaineering, situated at the end of the block. It's still there.

But one of the finest things I ever saw was at the Whole Coffee House located in the basement of Coffman Union, at the University on the East Bank. It was Rahsaan Roland Kirk. I was not familiar with his music then, but I was a Jethro Tull fan, and I knew Ian Anderson mimicked Kirk's discourse with the flute. Besides Anderson, Rahsaan was admired by all sorts of musicians, including rock and rollers like Frank Zappa and Jimi Hendrix. I wanted to see the source. It was quite the evening. Kirk stood up there in his golden robed regalia, a jazz priest with his talismans of horns and flutes draped about him, evoking the spirits of Blacknuss. He was quite a presence, and

38

you knew you were witnessing greatness. He had a wonderful rapport with his audience and was always throwing out some playful barbs. At some point, knowing this was Minnesota, he may have made a seemingly derogatory remark about Bob Dylan and folk music in general (being himself a champion of Black classical music, i.e. jazz). Some idiot white student started heckling him, asking what's wrong with Bob Dylan.

"Oh, I know who you are," Rahsaan said as he gazed out at the audience with his radar eyes behind those stoned blind sunglasses, "Oh, ahh, I don't see too well but I see you!"

Two Black dudes sitting in front of me started pounding on their table, guffawing and yelling, "It's too Black for Minneapolis! It's too Black for Minneapolis!"

Someone finally told the student to shut up and let the man play. It was too Black for Minneapolis. The irony is that Kirk was friends with so many musicians; I'd like to think he probably smoked dope with Dylan. This was in the fall of 1974. Sadly, Kirk would have his first stroke the next year—the year we went on the road.

Pigeon River

Jewell and I dropped out of the University of Minnesota in the spring of 1975; we would not be graduating that year. Instead, we camped at various sites north of the cities along the I-35 corridor, the route we would take for our great escape. We wanted to test our gear and break into it gradually to see how well it would go. I bought a pair of sturdy hiking boots and wore them every day to soften them up, slathering on plenty of mink oil for waterproofing. We also started having fights. I should have taken that as a sign that perhaps Jewell was having second thoughts. I knew that what we were about to do was not going to be a walk in the park. But this was a decision we had both made and a responsibility shared; I wasn't sure where all the contention was coming from. We were usually the happy couple and still new to each other. But every little thing I did was somehow irritating her. Jewell was watching me fiddle with our borrowed tent when a look of alarm gathered like a storm across her face.

40

"Watch what you're doing!"

"What?"

"You're breaking that branch!" I had sat on the lower branch of a pine tree next to our tent.

"Oh, yeah...sorry."

"And what a stupid thing—why did you cut the rope on the tent?"

"So...no one would trip on it?"

"Well, you never know when you could use a longer piece of rope."

"So...you tie it together again, so what?!"

"You're just so...insensitive," she said in her dismissive way. "Cutting things...breaking things..."

I think Jewell was coming unglued at the fomenting chaos about to envelope us. But I was also picking up a not-so-subtle hint of the general attitude that men were brutish and stupid. Being the feminist that she was, she always thought I needed some education on the subject. This was a common notion aimed at a lot of men at the time. Never mind that I was one of two guys in her Women's Literature class, or had the balls to even show up at the class party (Hey, where's that other guy?) and get cornered by a drunken woman who mouthed for me the lyrics to Yoko Ono's "Angry Young Woman" playing on the stereo (Embarrassing? Yes). But I agreed with the women's movement, which was good for both sexes, and made a concerted effort to examine my own hardwired notions of the role women played in society, especially in the arts.

Spring comes slowly in Minnesota. One day can tease you with its warmth and the next bring snow. I've seen the Duluth harbor frozen in June. But warmer days seemed to be at hand by the end of our spring quarter, and we knew it was time to get everything squared away with our apartment. This meant getting rid of what scant furniture and other forgettable possessions we had. A friend of ours brought over his van and helped us ship a large painting of mine to his girlfriend's attic in Edina. I have no idea what became of it. He also took my record collection, the only thing of mine that had any value besides the painting and stored it for me until we could find a home. The Dylan song, "Like a Rolling Stone," was playing on the radio and I heard the lyrics in a different way—as if it fit the moment perfectly. It was no longer a put down when he sang about being on your own, not having a home, and how does it feel, because it felt great.

Our friend Dawn was also planning a hitchhiking trip for the summer. She had acquired a dog for protection, although I'm not sure how great this lovable, shaggy, stinky mutt would do as a safeguard. Dawn was a talented flutist and would be graduating that year with a music degree. We talked of where we would like to go and what we might find once we got there. I realized I wasn't alone in my search for meaning in this life. We were all searchers. We were the artists: a writer, a musician, and a painter. Our initial plan was for the three of us (four, including Dog) to hitchhike together. But the more we looked at it the more preposterous it seemed. We stood on a lonely street corner in Minneapolis, with all our gear on, and took a hard look at one another. We had to split up. Who the hell's going to pick up a crowd? Hitching as a couple, however, might be a good strategy. We'd look like a starter kit for a family; Adam and Eve, just add an apple. So we had to say our goodbyes and watch Dawn walk away with her dog in tow. It would be a while before we saw her again.

And so here we were at a threshold. We dropped our letters of farewell to our parents with a scraping clunk into the mailbox and immediately felt a strange exhilaration of both fear and elation. We were done with the Midwest. After months of planning, our decision to leave family and friends behind had finally taken shape and now there was no turning back. Our declarations of independence from a prescribed life and all its obligations that our parents had expected us to fulfill would be received in a day or two and by then we would be long gone. After years of living with my mother and Elroy, I would be bidding them a not so fond farewell. Years of stress had left its mark on our relationship, and I was happy to finally have some control, however chaotic, over my own life. Writing this letter was not a difficult task for me other than trying my best to be diplomatic and to the point. As difficult as it was dealing with them, I vowed not to write an emotional letter. Perhaps it was a bit callous, but I had had enough. They wouldn't care about my feelings anyway. Writing it as impersonally as I could, would be the closest thing to a scalpel for making a clean cut. Or so I hoped.

Jewell's letter was more difficult to write. She had a strong connection with her mother and a fearful one with her father. She loved them both. I can't say that I loved mine, but I was empathetic with my mother.

"Mom will be upset when she reads we're hitchhiking," she said.

"But we'll be together. We're safer together than alone," I said.

"Dad will have a heart attack. Or he'll disown me for running off with you and us not being married."

"Really?"

"Probably. But they're my family. They'll come around eventually."

"What makes you think that?"

"Because they have to. We're young and have the advantage of time. Your parents will come around too, you'll see."

Interesting thought, but I doubted that. Jewell had actual parents. What I had was an emotionally disturbed mother and Elroy the Warden. Jewell also had a brother and a sister so there was more of a family dynamic going on. I was an only; a nervous actor in an unwelcome spotlight. But I was willing to believe that perhaps, in time, they would come around. Why not? Jewell was very persuasive and spoke with an authoritative nuance that she'd picked up from parents who were both teachers. The flipside of this is to sound like a know-it-all and Jewell was equally capable of that. She had a need to be domineering and, since my formative years were shaped by women, it was easy to acquiesce to her seeming authority. I needed to believe that everything would be okay, so for now,

I willingly took the bait. But on another level, I also knew that my mother was a typical hysteric and that she would not take it well. Elroy wouldn't care, other than having to deal with her crazy antics.

For us, or our friends, it wasn't such an unheard-of thing in the mid-1970s to take off like this. The Age of Aquarius was still rendering its blossoms of rebellion and we were part of the garden. But for our parents, who had lived through WWII and experienced certain deprivation, it must have seemed like we were just spoiled children throwing our lives away. Maybe we were. But there also comes a time when the fresh breeze of an open door beckons the sensate traveler to step outside. Like fledglings we had to open our wings and take a chance. It was *our* life now; what could go wrong?

Jewell and I boarded a train, with all that we owned on our backs, and headed for Duluth. It was late in the day and I didn't want to get stuck on the highway. Our packs were filled with camping gear, clothes, food, and a couple of books, which didn't help in the weight department. The books I brought were the *I Ching* and Henry James' *The Americans*. I wanted to bring the *I Ching* along because I thought it might be useful when faced with major decisions while on the road. I thought it might be smart, or at least a poetic gesture, to use a system based on chance for reading the chance experiences that befell us, especially in terms of direction, by tossing the coins and referring to the hexagrams for guidance. Why not? When you have nothing, you have nothing to lose. It would be our cosmic compass. I purchased the version John Cage had recommended when I spoke to him at a concert he gave earlier that year. Cage, and the dancer Merce Cunningham, used chance operations to determine composition in their respective pieces. I brought the Henry James along because I had so much trouble reading him. I thought maybe I'd magically get smart between rides if I forced myself to read it. Of course, I ended up tossing it by the wayside. I also brought along my journal so I could record everything. I soon found that life on the road was sometimes too hectic to write down what happened and that some moments would be reduced to only a few good sticks of broken memory.

When we pulled into Duluth, I called my friend Billy and asked if he could pick us up and let us crash on his floor. He was there in a moment with his newly purchased van. It was one of those "love-boats" that had blue shag carpeting throughout, including the ceiling, with a mattress in the back and a nice set of speakers. Billy was a strange cat—long fiery red hair and a long straight nose. We used to do acid together and had shared an apartment with three other people when I was going to UMD. He wasn't a student like the rest of us, so his private life was a little different from ours. I don't remember how it was that he came to live among us but we were all from "Woodstock Nation" so it mattered little.

We hadn't eaten since breakfast, so Billy asked us where we'd like to go for dinner.

"Oh man, we have to do Sandy's," I said. Billy let out a laugh.

"What's so funny about Sandy's?" Jewell asked.

"When Billy and I lived with all those other freaks we'd get stoned and meander into Sandy's just to watch their staff open the door for you, dressed in these ridiculous Scottish uniforms, and say, 'Welcome to Sandy's.' You could barely keep from laughing; they were so eager beaver phony and so young. And then we'd all tumble to the counter, with our glazed-over eyes, and try to make sense of the menu, which was pretty straight forward really, but we were anything but straight."

"Yeah, they don't open the door for you anymore." Billy smiled.

"Yeah, I know. Hey, remember that girl, Louise, who lived with us? She'd order a burger with fries and then put the fries inside the bun for a big mouthful of grease!"

"Sandy's it is then," said Billy as he floored the van up one of Duluth's impossibly steep hills.

After dinner we drove over to Ray's Movilla on the UMD campus. These were housing units that looked like fancy trailers; Ray had moved out of the dorms and lived in one of these for his senior year. By chance, Larry was there too and we all had a good time reminiscing about our acid adventures. I was happy for them; they'd all be graduating and moving on to the next logical thing. But I was also a bit sad, and even a little jealous, about the prescribed life Jewell and I had so resolutely rejected that would be enjoyed by my old comrades. We slept in Billy's van that night. In the morning we had breakfast at Jerry Lee's Truck Stop, and then Billy dropped us off at the northern outskirts of town.

We got a few local rides up the shore with not too much trouble. The weather was beautiful and golden. All of our worries about the future were suspended in the face of this grand adventure. The day was filled with a profound silence, punctuated only by the occasional hissing of passing cars, and the air was filled with the scent of northern pines—that distinct and very heady turpentine-earth-honey smell that only seems to exist on the North Shore. The downwardly spiraling trills of a veery also kept us company. Everything was so gorgeous, and so fine, and so right *now* that I felt too small and inexperienced to appreciate it in its fullness. Hitchhiking, one of life's little accelerants, was rapidly becoming my new drug. What would it show us? I just wanted to embrace the world and be done with myself and my irritating penchant for self-doubt.

We stayed in a cheap motel that evening, not too far from the Canadian border. Our plan was to hitch into Canada and take the Trans-Canada Highway, the same one Sam and I took four years ago, across the great expanse to the West Coast. We had five hundred dollars between us in traveler's checks.

The next morning, we got a ride from a very chatty Canadian and crossed over at Pigeon River. It felt a little peculiar going into another country as a hitchhiker, but it wasn't like crossing into Mexico where you would need a visa; I'd been back and forth many times.

"I don't know," I said. "Do you think the border guards care if we're hitchhikers?"

"Oh, they won't care; people hitch all over in Canada," said our driver.

We pulled into the station, not knowing what to expect. Why should we expect anything other than a short lull in our journey?

A fat guard with a bushy mustache came over and had us get out of the car. He waddled around, ordered the trunk to be opened, gazed at the tires, and then had us make our declarations.

"Just going home to Thunder Bay," said our cheery driver.

"And what about you two? Going home to Thunder Bay too?"

"No sir, we're from the U.S., hitchhiking to Vancouver and then south along the coast."

"You're not Canadian?" He started eyeing us and me especially, because of how I looked with my few days of beard growth and hair that hung down my back. He rifled through our packs. We had to lay out every goddamn piece and parcel of our gear and line it up on the filthy sidewalk. Finally, he found what he was looking for—a bottle of Tylenol with suspicious content, i.e., two kinds of small white pills, one with a stamped logo and the other plain. Jewell had combined two different brands of acetaminophen for the sake of compression in our worldly goods.

"Okay, you're free to go." He pointed to our ride—who looked back at us rather fearfully. He probably thought he had just dodged a bullet and would never pick up another hitchhiker, especially in the States.

"You two come with me."

We were marched into the building. The other guards were all young and had these pleasant plastic smiles. Everybody was friendly except Captain Kangaroo's evil twin. "All right, we're gonna search 'em," he said. Jewell was taken by a couple of women while the walrus and another young fool took me to a side room.

"Okay, take off your clothes ... all of 'em ... bend over and spread 'em." I was shaking while a flashlight desired to be a colonoscopy.

"What are these marks on your arm?" He pointed to the dark brown spots on my forearm.

"They're moles." I couldn't believe what was happening.

He reached into one of the pockets of my shirt, pulled out some cellophane that once housed a cookie, and pointing to the crumbs said, "What's this?"

"Cookie crumbs."

"Okay, get your clothes on. We've checked out your so-called Tylenol and it tests as amphetamine."

"What? That's insane! What kind of fucking bullshit is this?!" Fear had turned to rage. The guard had a sly and bemused smile; he was gloating in his power.

"We've called in a constable from Thunder Bay; he'll take you into custody."

Jewell had gone through the same humiliations and was in a near state of tears. The acetaminophen tested as amphetamine on their rinky-dink chemistry set, provided for all Canadian space cadets. And so we were being charged with possession of an illegal substance and entering a foreign country with intent to traffic since we were carrying a full bottle. Expectations of a free and unfettered slide across the country quickly became darkened by the promise of a cage and God-knows-what-else for our indiscernible future. I was afraid we weren't going to be free for some time. Here was our grand entrance into Canada.

51

Thunder Bay

When the constable finally pulled up all the young guards stood in formation, wearing their plastic smiles again. I'd like to think they also looked rather sorry. Obviously, fatso was running the show. The constable put us and our gear into his car and off we went to Thunder Bay. The chemical sample of our Tylenol, kept in a plastic test tube, was starting to dissolve the tube and burn into his shirt pocket, leaking onto his chest. We told him of our innocence, and he was quite chatty and upbeat while trying to disengage the sticky liquid from his clothing.

At the station, I was led to a counter where they muddied our fingers with ink for posterity. "We're innocent," I said, "Why are you taking our fingerprints?"

"It's just a formality. Don't worry, they'll get tossed after your court date," our constable said. I didn't believe him.

They took me down the hall and put me in jail. It was just like in the movies: gray walls, stainless steel toilet, shitty bed, showers across the way. I could hear Jewell somewhere, bawling her eyes out. It looked like I would have to spend the weekend there since it was a late Friday afternoon and the bondsman had gone home. I didn't know what they were going to do with Jewell. They took away my belt and shoes. I guess they didn't want me to hang myself for possession of aspirin. I don't know why they took my shoes—maybe for fear I'd use them as a deadly weapon. I was in a parallel universe with Arlo Guthrie and his "Alice's Restaurant Massacree," but nothing was funny.

Prisoners had managed one way or another to scrawl their names on the walls and ceiling. A guy named "Butch" wrote his name with cigarette smoke directly over my head. Someone else used the same technique to draw a ghostly primitive nude. Ah, the delicate technique of fumage; these contemporary dwellers of the Lascaux caves were alive and well. Meanwhile, Jewell's wailing had taken on a life of its own. You could really hear it bouncing off the barren cell walls. Our constable came back to me and said he was able to get ahold of their bondsman—we could post bail at a hundred dollars apiece and then come into court on Monday morning. They were going to send the test samples to Winnipeg where it would take a month for the results. If the test was negative, we'd get our money back; if positive, we would be extradited to Canada to face trial. Jewell stopped crying. I don't think we would have gotten this reprieve if she hadn't raised the tears to an epic proportion. So the two hundred dollar total bail reduced our resources to two hundred seventy dollars; we wouldn't see that money for a while. We were free to go; see you next week.

Our constable gave us a ride out to Kakabeka Falls Park where we camped for two nights. The Canadian cops seemed so much nicer than the ones in the States. The scenery was beautiful, but being captive, who could enjoy it? We got a ride back into Thunder Bay on Sunday from a couple of hippies; guys of British descent who had rather extravagant accents. They sounded very rough, almost Cockney. The side doors of their van slid open and they pulled us in. ZZ Top was on the 8-track. They were coming down from an all-night acid trip— tired, rugged eyes still glowing from paradise. They offered to sell us a tab but we declined. Then they started passing a joint and we said no to that too. "No drugs, hey?" asked the driver. We told them of our plight and they were incensed—sick and tired of the "establishment." "Fek 'em!" they cried.

"Hey, you dig Zed Zed Tope? I really...oh God...I rilly dig Zed Zed. They're so...God...they just kick the snot outta it!"

I laughed; everything he said was getting the snot kicked out of it. I told him, "Yeah...I like ZZ Top." When they dropped us off, the snot kicker wished us well on our journey and told us not to worry about court on Monday. His final words were, what else, "Hey mon, kick the snot outta it!"

We found our way to a Holiday Inn that was just around the corner from the courts; another fifteen bucks out the window. After a cheap "McSupper" of burgers and fries we settled into our room.

54

"Those guys who dropped us off were pretty funny," Jewell said.

"Yeah, can you imagine if we dropped acid and then showed up at court tomorrow?" I laughed.

"I can't imagine dropping acid if we weren't."

"You've never done it have you?" I asked.

"No, I was always afraid to. I'd be afraid of acting crazy and then getting picked up by the cops."

"It's not like that," I said. "You know how beautiful fall colors can be, all those fluorescent orange and pink leaves tinged in bronze...how even more magical they are in the twilight, with shadows stretching like an eternity across the lawn?"

"Yeah, so?"

"So did you go around screaming and acting crazy because of how beautiful everything is? Acid, for most people, is like that. You're just quietly in awe."

"Well, you hear stories."

"Yeah, I guess you do. I think people who are doing it on a lark get into trouble."

"So you never did it for a lark?"

"No. I knew it was serious stuff. I did it 'cause it was better than suicide and I had nothing to lose. God and the devil are in your head," I said. "The trick is to let yourself go; the ego carries too much baggage. I mean, really, you have to trust that there's nothing worth holding onto."

"What about chromosome damage? Aren't you afraid of having kids now?"

"That was all bullshit; journalists making up scary stories for their readership to spice up their miserable lives. You damage about as many chromosomes drinking a cup of coffee."

"How do you know...where'd you hear that?"

"Ray told me. And he heard it from his dad, a doctor."

I pulled off my boots and stretched out on the bed, gazing up at the sparkled popcorn ceiling that glinted like an absurd snowbank. We were both pretty tired and anxious for tomorrow's outcome. Jewell fluffed her pillow and settled in. She was familiar with most of my acid stories, but I started reviving them again just to pass the time. Reminiscing is a good way to calm yourself down. One thing that really stuck in my memory was experiencing synesthesia. I had split a tab with Billy and was sitting in the front seat of his car listening to a Bach fugue on the radio. It was night and we were driving into Duluth. I noticed the fugue was getting louder but when I looked at the radio it wasn't on. Where was this music coming from? I looked out the window and saw that as we came closer to a Clark gas station—with its huge round orange and white sign and circling lights—that the music was coming from the sign! The lights were going around and around, generating a Bach fugue. I even heard a Doppler effect as we passed it.

Another experience involving synesthesia was hearing the sun come up. After tripping all night, I had crawled wearily into bed for some shut eye when I heard sitar music being played. It was a very mellow raga, like all ragas start out.

I thought someone had put a Ravi Shankar record on the turntable downstairs, but everyone was asleep. Then I noticed that the music was getting louder as the twilight of dawn infused my window. I was quite amazed. As the rosy light got brighter, the raga faded and morphed into what sounded like thousands of voices. It was the sound of humanity. Finally, the sun cleared the horizon and the voices dissipated into the gold and silvery light of day. I was sorry to see the enchantment end.

"Wow, that's pretty intense; I guess you were pretty lucky with all that drug stuff."

"There were some spooky trips as well," I said.

I told her of prowling about in the dead of a winter's night with my friend Ted who was also tripping. We stumbled into an all-night Coney Island for a bite to eat. I wasn't hungry. I was never hungry on acid for some reason; food, and the act of eating, just seemed gross. But Ted was hungry, so he went to order, and I was going to find us a booth. I poked into the darkness when, all of a sudden, this man stood up from one of the booths, looked at me and said, "What?!" I *knew* he was fresh from an asylum. He was crazy and I was on the same level, albeit artificially, as he was. I promptly turned around and went out the door.

Ted came out with a mouthful of hotdog and said, "What's up?"

I explained what had happened. Now, whenever I remember that incident, I always think of that David Bowie song, "The Bewlay Brothers," whose lyrics capture the dark mystery and psychosis of that experience.

"Maybe you were doing something weird and didn't realize it."

"Nah. I was always completely aware of myself and my surroundings."

Jewell looked dubious. "Who was Ted?"

"He was a writer and a musician; played the clarinet. You never met him." I told her of the group of people Billy and I lived with and how we were invited over for a small party at Ted's parents' house. He was house-sitting for them. We all dropped acid and trooped over. Ted had dropped earlier, and when we rang the doorbell, he took one look at us and told us to get the hell out of here, slamming the door in our face. We all looked at each other dumbfounded.

"Boy, he's really weird," said one.

"Yeah, what's gotten into him?" said another.

We were about to turn around and leave when I thought to try once more. I told the mob to back off and rang the doorbell again. Ted opened the door and looked at me.

"Yes?"

"Hi Ted," I said. "Could I come in?"

"Sure, that would be just fine," he said and very cordially invited me in. "I'm really sorry. I was watching TV when the picture started to melt and drift around the room and then all of a sudden all you people are ringing the damn doorbell. I just freaked."

"How about if we let them in one at a time?" I suggested.

58

We went back to the door and let them in one by one. Later, a friend of his dropped by, a character we all knew as an acid casualty—a very burned-out person who was always on something. He could go through a lid of pot by himself in a couple of days. I didn't like, and always avoided, this guy and he knew it. So when he showed up at this party, I glanced at him in my drugged state and *saw* for an instant what he truly was. He was faceless. I was looking at the raw meat of the front of his head as if someone had sliced it right off. My subconscious was telling me there's no one there and I just couldn't look at him. Thankfully he disappeared after a while. But word got out in the neighborhood that there was a party going on and pretty soon all sorts of people showed up—some underage—and Ted was not happy about it. Folks just kept piling in and it felt like we were in the middle of a Fellini movie. There were even a couple of dwarfs running around like servants grabbing beers out of the fridge for anyone who asked.

The most frightening experience, however, was being bitten by my girlfriend. Someone had brought a liquor sampler, one of those mini-liquor bottles, filled with water and eighteen hits of blotter to a party we were having. I have no idea what the dosage was for each hit but there were only seven of us and we drained the thing. We each took one small sip except for my girlfriend, who not being able to comprehend the gravity of this mini bottle, took two sips. I don't remember what the circumstances were, but later, at some point when we were all "peaking," I noticed that her teeth were sunk into my arm; a bright purplish light was traveling from that spot, up my arm like a slow burning fuse. It took at least four seconds for that bright gob of light to get to my brain, to let me know there was some pain going on, and that perhaps I ought to do something about it—like pull away. She was having a freak-out, as they say. Of course, the next day, she didn't remember any of it. Perhaps she was expressing her dissatisfaction with our relationship; we broke up shortly after that. All she remembered about the trip was giving birth to hundreds of people while simultaneously watching them die.

But all things, as they say, must come to an end. The last time I tripped was with someone I didn't know very well and found myself in the role of caretaker. It made me feel incredibly ancient—not a good feeling when you're nineteen or twenty years old. I felt like I was one of those figures in a Chinese landscape where the people are small and the landscape overwhelming. I took it as a sign that it was time to quit. And, anyway, I didn't want to end up like "Faceless." After leaving it alone for a while I started to wonder: what the hell was I doing? I must have been crazy! The shackles of Plato's Cave were willingly reinstated, and I never did it again.

After my rambling monologue, I looked over at Jewell who had dropped off into an enviable slumber; my talk of psychedelics had put her to sleep. I guess it was like telling someone your dreams; no one is interested in them but you. I couldn't blame her; it was an exhausting day. I turned off the lights, but I was too upset to sleep. I paced around the motel room wondering at our fate. Who knew what would happen next? I just wanted to get it over with. I hardly slept that night.

In the morning we walked over to the courts where we met our public defender, a short guy in a suit with horn-rimmed glasses, and told him the whole story. He groaned. There were a number of cases ahead of us consisting of local ne'er-do-wells all lined up on a bench against the wall. They were mostly young and mostly there on charges of disorderly conduct, drunken driving, car stealing, and possession of marijuana. The white-haired judge was very firm, seemed to know some of the culprits from before, and handed out his jurisdictions accordingly to a grumbling ruckus of recipients. Our case was next. We stood up and the lawyer approached the bench.

"Your Honor, these young folks from the States are travelling through our fair country, hoping to build a life for themselves in California, etc."

I was impressed—this guy deserved an Oscar. The judge looked at the papers set before him. He winced. Then he put his head down, rubbing it slowly with his hand.

"Is this report from that same border guard as last week?"

"Yes sir, I believe so."

"Dammit...that's the third time this month!"

Apparently, this border guard was aiming to make the drug bust of the year and all of it phony, tying up the court's time and resources. I don't think he was doing himself any favors with this judge. Our trial was set for September. By that time the acetaminophen will have been tested and the warrant removed. We were free to go.

We had breakfast near the motel and then got a ride to the outskirts of town, back to Kakabeka Falls and then another straight shot up onto the Trans-Canada. All our rides had been local; it hardly seemed worth it to be tossing our heavy packs in and out of cars but at least we were moving.

"Well, we finally made it to Highway One," I said.

"Do you think we should be going ahead with this?" was Jewell's reply.

"What do you mean? Are you kidding?"

"Almost half our money is gone! Maybe we should go back and live in Duluth…"

I couldn't believe what I was hearing. It was true though, we had lost so much of our travel money that I couldn't be sure how long we'd be able to stay on the road. I quite naively thought five dollars a day could do it—we were now averaging ten dollars a day, not counting the loss of the bail money that took out forty percent of our resources.

"No. We're not going back. We've already made a decision to do this. There's no going back. Look, we can do this. We'll sleep by the side of the road if we have to." I could see Jewell's need to be dominant all the time beginning to fade. Being tired, and reflecting on what we just went through, was undermining that commanding will of hers.

"Look at what a bright beautiful day this is. All we need is a good ride."

"Okay…"

"Besides, wouldn't it be funny if we went through Pigeon River again? We could say hello to you-know-who."

Jewell smirked. "Hilarious."

And our next ride was pretty good; a middle-aged guy who took us for about four hundred and five kilometers (roughly two hundred and fifty miles) passing through all these little towns: Mokomon, Shabaqua Raith, Ignace, Dinorwic, Wabigoon, and Dryden. Nothing but eternal evergreens, punctuated by "jewelry" and other trinket shops, with a crystal blue sky hanging over our heads. We were happy to leave Thunder Bay far behind. Our driver was curious about us and wished he were young again with not a care in the world. If he only knew! He dropped us off at Vermilion Bay in the early afternoon. We made some peanut butter sandwiches from the meager supplies we kept on hand for emergencies and kept thumbing.

The Canadian Prairies

We were munching our sandwiches when a rusty station wagon pulled up with four people in it. The car held one Frenchman from Quebec, two from Manitoba, and a driver of British descent who was from Nova Scotia. Derrick, our driver, was a bit rotund and had brown curly hair, blue-gray eyes and a horseshoe mustache. The two Frenchmen were father and son, itinerant welders returning for more work in Winnipeg. I never did catch their names. They were very quiet and serene with their long hair, sad sunken eyes, and gallant noses. The other Frenchman, Richard, was a short swarthy guy with black hair and almost black eyes. He was headed for Banff. All of them were hitchhikers that Derrick had picked up as he wound his way across the country. And now there were six of us crammed into the car with all of our gear piled up in the back.

After a few miles I noticed a small pull-off along the highway that looked like a bus stop out in the middle of nowhere. I pointed to it and asked, "Derrick, what are these bus stops with the shelters doing way out here?"

"Those are hitchhiking stations."

"Are you kidding?"

"Yeah, they're off to the side so driver and rider can safely maneuver. We have them all over on Highway One."

"Wow. You won't find that in the States."

Derrick smiled.

"So where are you headed?" I asked.

"I'm going to Revelstoke, on the other side of the Rockies."

We drove for hours, winding around through endless verdant hills of primordial forests and turquoise lakes. No one was saying much; we were just contented travelers, happy to be on our respective ways. After a while, Winnipeg came into view and Derrick was kind enough to drop father and son off wherever they needed to be. They seemed to know approximately where they were headed, having done this a couple of times. We wished them luck and then sprinted west out of the city, onto the prairie lit by a blazing orange sunset, the sky striped with long bands of lavender. David Bowie's *Rebel Rebel* came on the radio. Jewell wondered if there were any campsites along the way and if we should start looking for one. I was wondering that too since it was starting to get dark, the night fast on our heels behind us.

"I don't know of any," said Derrick. "We can keep an eye open. There might be a KOA along here somewhere."

65

"Why would you want to get out? Why not go all night?" Richard asked, "You'll never get another ride like this."

"Yeah," Derrick said. "I'm going straight through tonight. I hate the prairies. It's best to do them at night and then by morning it's not too far to the mountains."

Yes, it seemed obvious. We would go all night—all the way to the Canadian Rockies! Now that there was more room we could spread out in the car. Jewell and Richard stretched out in back while Derrick and I would trade off with the driving. The first quarter moon was on the rise as twilight overtook us. We went through Brandon, Virden, Elkhorn, then crossed from Manitoba into Saskatchewan and on through Moosomin, Indian Head, Regina, Moose Jaw, Swift Current... And we were in a swift current, stopping only for coffee, food, and a piss; filling up on gas (everyone chips in) and pouring another quart of oil into our leaking heap of a caravan. We only experienced about an hour or two of total darkness that night—our latitude keeping us in perpetual twilight. The sun's presence disturbed the horizon ever so slightly, staying just below the ridge of the earth. It made you feel like it wasn't quite time to go to sleep (helped, of course, by the coffee). It was then that I had what Sam would have called a cosmic truth from the road. It was that everything was round, the earth was round, the sun and moon were round, their orbits were round and their light was rounding up from the rounded shoulders of the Earth; that we were round, our wheels were round, in fact our life was a cycle, and we etched our flight in a curvilinear path that sizzled on the circumference of this

66

planet. It was a simple ineffable truth, a stoner's truth, where words could easily be replaced by images of spirals, gyres, and cycles. Even the stars that seemed so fixed were moving, if ever so slowly, in their own vortices. And weren't we moving with them, or against them, and aren't we all just expanding out from the biggest and oldest ball of an explosion whose birth was so small as to not have had any shape or dimension, and whose destiny may not have a shape unless it blossoms onto another bubble, another sphere, beyond our comprehension? I began to feel very small realizing one clear thing, and that was: *movement is round.*

Jewell and Richard seemed to be having a good time talking in the back seat until, suddenly, she came vaulting over the front seat.

"He tried to make out with me," she said in a low voice. I turned and looked at Richard who had a sort of "so what?" look on his face. An oppressive silence now filled the car. Mr. Macho now had the back seat all to himself. Derrick, in an effort to ameliorate the weird vibe hanging in the air, decided to start singing some traditional British drinking songs. He had dozens of them and began soloing to keep our spirits up. The melodies were from old sea shanties. He'd teach us the chorus and we'd pipe in. Richard fell asleep in the back, lulled by a rocking car and the lullabies of tired sailors:

> *Well it's all for me grog, me jolly jolly grog,*
> *It's all for me beer and tobacco.*

For I spent all me tin on the lassies drinking gin,
Far across the western ocean I must wander.

Where are me boots, me noggin', noggin' boots,
They're all gone for beer and tobacco.
For the heels are worn out and the toes are kicked about
And the soles are looking out for better weather.

Well it's all for me grog, me jolly jolly grog,
It's all for me beer and tobacco.
For I spent all me tin on the lassies drinking gin,
Far across the western ocean I must wander.

After a while, we were all getting so tired it was hard to remember how the chorus' went. Even Derrick was beginning to nod, hypnotized by our headlights glowing into the nothingness of the onrushing highway.

"Would you mind taking over the wheel?" he said, looking in my direction.

"Not at all."

"Let's do a stop up ahead then and switch places." There was an all-night truck stop lighting up the horizon of the not-too-distant future.

"Sounds good."

We pulled over, gassed up, and made our ablutions. Derrick climbed into the backseat with Richard and propped himself against the window, jacket bunched for a pillow. I got into the driver's seat and tore across the gravel, back to our epic ride.

"It was so still out there," Jewell said.

"I know. I noticed it too," I said. "What time is it? Three? Four?"

"Who knows," she said. "I brought everything but a watch."

"Should we turn the car around and go back to Pigeon River?" I asked.

"Ha! Wouldn't Derrick and Richard be surprised?" She snickered.

"We could say hello to that fat ass guard again and ask him for the time."

"Yeah, or we could bring him some Tylenol; he's going to need it when he hears from that judge. You were right...I'm so glad we kept going," Jewell said. "And anyway, what's time? We're on our own time now."

"Ah, you're having a cosmic truth, are you? A road truth," I said.

"Yeah?"

"I was having one myself back there...while we were headed into the night. It was simply that 'movement was round'...or something like that."

"Is that an empirical truth or a subjective truth?" Jewell loved to joust.

"Empirical truths don't exist," I said, "only subjective ones."

"Isn't it an empirical truth that everyone dies?" she said.

"It's not empirical to the one who's dying; it's only empirical to the ones who are living, which is to say it's only an observation not an experience. Death is subjective…and the dead know nothing of it."

"I never thought of you as an atheist," she said.

"I never thought of myself as anything," I said.

"So, you don't believe in anything."

"Not like all your church-going friends you grew up with, if that's what you mean. And anyway…'belief' is a stupid word. You either know something or you don't." I was being rather glib; it was self-defense. I hated talking about beliefs, because really, what does it prove? I believed in my own intuition, or in anyone else's for that matter. Intuition wrought the fire that kept intellect warm.

We were quiet for a while; nothing but the endless whoosh of wheels propelling us to our destiny and a vague sense of expectation that arises from being in the moment.

"Is it getting lighter?" Jewell said.

"I can't tell. I don't think it ever got completely dark," I said.

Jewell pointed to the horizon. "I'm seeing some hills…over there."

An almost imperceptible grayness began to filter across our view; the curtain of night was lifting. I had never actually seen a prairie before and here it was, in all its treeless glory, stretching further into infinity as the sun rose.

The needle on the gas gauge was dipping slowly towards the quarter tank mark and I was a little anxious to find a station soon. We rolled into one a half-hour later, just in time. Derrick fumbled his way from a dream. "Hmm...where...what's up...oh, man..."

"Got some sleep, did you?" I asked.

"Oh, yeah, man that was great...thanks. Where are we?"

"You'd know better than us...and we need gas."

Everyone got out and stretched their legs. I couldn't believe all the sounds and smells! The air was so fresh, and there seemed to be hundreds of birds—none I'd ever heard before. All you could see were these rolling hills of grass. The prairie was a full-throated song; the distant hills seemed to echo that song in a visual ululation. I guess for Derrick it was a bore, but I will never forget the power of this landscape seen at dusk with no sleep. I thought it was the most beautiful thing—mostly because it was so foreign and, like Dorothy, I knew I wasn't in Kansas anymore. Derrick got back into the driver's seat, and we peeled out onto the King's Highway once again.

The sun went from sanguine to gold—the alchemy of morning. By this time, we were all getting hungry and looking for a place to have breakfast. Somewhere outside of Medicine Hat we spotted a diner that was surrounded by a barrage of dusty rusty pickups. We figured it to be a pretty good place for food so we parked on the outside of the lot and marched in. I noticed most of the trucks had gun racks and bumper stickers: THE DAY THEY TAKE AWAY MY GUN IS THE DAY THEY PRY MY COLD DEAD FINGER FROM THE TRIGGER. I didn't know Canada had a second amendment, and indeed they don't. But the "Bungalow Bills" of this world are everywhere; no need to hide behind a second amendment. Still, I had no idea there were Canadian cowboys—all hats and boots. There was virtually no difference between this mob and anyone you'd see down in the Western States.

A noisy clatter of voices and breakfast plates greeted us as we made our way through the smoke of bacon, sausages, and cigarettes; an early morning sun slicing through the haze. We found an open table and settled in. There were quite a few eyes riveted in our direction. We were three long haired guys and a girl all looking rather disheveled and frazzled. What were a bunch of hippies doing out here at their watering hole? This was at a time when anyone with long hair wasn't just embracing a fashion—it was a damn statement. We were anti-establishment, nonconformists, bohemians all. Let your freak flag fly. The three of us were feeling uncomfortable with shades of *Easy Rider* in the back of our collective minds, but Richard, our Frenchman, couldn't give a crap. "Ahh, luke ad dzhem, dzhose focking anarcheests," he mocked, simultaneously voicing the thoughts of the cowboy crowd. We all got coffee and when the waitress came back to take our orders everyone but Richard ordered omelets. He had brought his rucksack and proceeded to fish out a piece of bread along with a jar of peanut butter. As the waitress pitched the omelets around our table he looked up at her while slathering his bread and said, "Yew 'av' viry gude peenoot booter." He was really laying on the French accent and we all giggled. I thought he was going to get himself, or us, thrown out of there. But nothing happened. The steely stares from the other customers

72

just became more numerous and steadier. Breakfast finished, we stumbled through the chairs and tables to the cashier and made our getaway.

By midmorning we were approaching Calgary, passing through its ugly miles of motels. The weather had changed from the golden plains to a chilly rain. We could tell we were entering the mountains. When we stopped for gas, another ragged hippie approached the car, wanting a ride.

"Hey man, can you give me a ride into town?"

"Sure, hop in," said Derrick.

"Hey, it's a car full of creepy crawlers. Where you all headed? Where you from? My name's Alex. Can you spare me some change? I'm not prejudice; I'll take American, ha ha ha ha ha." The guy was a bit obnoxious, and I was sorry Derrick let him in. He was very erratic and overpowering—obviously a speed freak—acting like he owned the car, and us, and wanted to be dropped off at some specific place in town. Derrick told him he wasn't deviating from our route. We dropped him somewhere on the highway in the middle of town.

Heading west, we could see an island of clouds on the horizon, but we weren't really paying attention until suddenly, after turning a corner, the Canadian Rockies came into view, looming through the mist. I had never seen anything so absolute. There they were, complete with snowcaps, jutting out of the terrain as if some giant had thrown them there. Their steely blue presence was so strong, and seemed so impossible, I felt I could almost hear them—that if you took a giant hammer and struck them, they wouldn't crumble but would instead resonate like a bell or a Tibetan singing bowl.

"Wow, these are quite impressive," I said.

"Yeah, they're a little different than the ones you've got in the States," Derrick said.

"Yeah? How? Are they bigger?"

"I don't know about bigger…just a lot more jagged looking."

"They look like big blue wolf teeth," said Jewell.

"They're even more beautiful in Jasper," said Richard. "The ones in the States are just foothills." Richard was doing his swagger again. Derrick looked at him funnily in the rear view. "Not so sure about that, buddy," he said, "But, yeah, Jasper's pretty special."

Banff was coming up soon and so some decisions had to be made: stay with Derrick through the mountains or stop at Banff for a while? We were all exhausted and needed sleep. Richard said the camping was great there, so Jewell and I decided we'd do some sightseeing and camp there too. Derrick dropped off the three of us on the outskirts of town and drove on; our non-stop express had come to an end. We had made it to Banff from Vermillion Bay in about twenty hours.

Richard drifted off and set up his tent down inside a shallow ravine, not too far from the road, forgoing the family campgrounds. That was the last we saw of him; no goodbyes. We set up camp a little further down the road. We were too exhausted for much else.

Gentleman of the Road

That evening I pulled out the *I Ching*. I wasn't really too familiar with it, and there wasn't any need to consult it for direction since Highway One was our default route; there was no quicker way to the West Coast nor were we having to make any big decisions as to what direction to take. We knew where we were going. I understood the basic premise of this book, and the Chinese view of reality, from reading Carl Jung's forward. The Eastern view is that reality was occurring *in the moment* and not, as in Western tradition, the sum of a causal chain of events. The Western mind loves to measure and make a statistical generalization about observed nature while the Eastern mind takes nature as a whole, in the moment, complete with the minutest deviations. One need only look at a classical Greek statue to understand this is the body perfected, and not reality. Chance has a different connotation to the Western mind than it does to the Eastern. For the Chinese, the interpretation of chance events occurring in the moment gives a better understanding of reality, as it includes everything, rather than the hypothetical reasons for the chain of events observed by the Western mind. And part of this inclusion of events, in any given moment, is the person consulting the *I Ching*, for the individual is just as much a part of any given moment as anything else.

The oracle is obtained, traditionally, by tossing and "reading" the outcome of forty-nine scattered yarrow stalks. That sounded pretty elaborate, and I didn't have any yarrow stalks on me...not that I knew what a yarrow stalk was. Thankfully, there was a quicker method that involved the tossing and interpreting of three Chinese coins. I didn't have any Chinese coins either. But, I did have three U.S. pennies. The sides of the coins have a numerical value of two and three; two for yin and three for yang. So I made tails yin and heads yang. Now all I needed was a predicament.

Gentleman of the Road

We weren't sure where to go so we strode into town for a looksee. Banff was a cozy little burg with a long main street and a few hotels. We walked into one and inquired where the best places for hiking and camping were. The guy at the front desk mentioned several campsites, and said that if we really wanted to do some serious hiking to head up the road towards Lake Minnewanka. We wanted serious. He also told us that Aylmer Lookout was a destination for a lot of hikers and that it was on the same trail as the campsites. We picked up some victuals and headed out to the Lake Minnewanka parking lot. The map at the trailhead revealed a primitive campsite about six miles away. It was gorgeous rugged country and the weather was fine. Snow-capped mountains plunged into a lake colored only by glacial silt in a soft cyan. White mountain goats dotted the sides of the valley; spectral denizens on a vertical sweep. We stopped for a drink at a stream. I had never tasted water of such purity before or since. It was sweet and

77

powerful and looked like liquid glass. The trail took an abrupt turn as we walked into a surprising wall of odor—a very pungent barnyard smell. What was this barnyard smell doing out here? A few more steps gave us the answer: not more than ten feet away was a huge mountain sheep, a bighorn ram. Neither of us had ever seen anything like this, and so close, that wasn't in a zoo. I freaked out and suggested to Jewell in a whisper that we should be calm, sit down very slowly, and turn our backs to the animal. I figured if we had our backs to it, the backpacks would cushion any blow should he decide to charge. We sat very still. The animal was very still. We sat some more. The sheep continued chewing its cud. After sitting for maybe fifteen minutes, and feeling rather foolish, we stood up and left. Other than grazing, the ram hardly moved or even noticed us; he didn't care. Later, when we came back from camp, we saw tourists feeding a flock of these guys in the parking lot.

By late afternoon we had set up our tent at the first campsite on the trail. It was situated on a beach of large stones and scattered driftwood. There was a wooden latrine, a picnic table, a fire pit and that's about all. We were the only ones there. It was starting to get chilly so we built a fire and made plans to climb the lookout on the next day. But the next day was filled with freezing sheets of rain. We were stuck in the tent forever—couldn't even get a fire started, so hot meals were not forthcoming. We ate granola. Our third day out was not much better, but the rain let up a little so we decided to try for Aylmer Lookout but turned back when we discovered some rather large bear tracks. We did not want to be around bears this time of year due to the possibility of meeting momma bear with her cubs. Also, the rain was returning and would stay with us for the rest of the day. We ate more granola. To pass the time in our frigid tent, I made a small chess board in the back of my journal and tore out a page for the construction of tiny chess pieces. Miniscule pebbles in confusing shades of light and dark became pawns. It was hard to keep track of all these little pieces and so the game kept our attention for about twenty minutes. We were getting on each other's nerves.

Jewell asked, "Why do you keep grunting?"

"Huh? I didn't know I was grunting."

"Every time you get up or move around you go, 'unh'."

"Well, I guess I'm tired," I sighed.

"And you keep sighing every two minutes."

"Well, I guess I'll shut up then, Christ!"

"I'm hungry."

"Have some granola."

"I'm sick of eating granola!"

There wasn't much to the granola bag at this point anyway since I had picked out all the good stuff; all that was left was a lot of raw oatmeal and unrecognizable bits of sweetness. It kept us pretty regular though.

On the fourth day, the rain let up and a ranger came ashore to check on any campers who might be there. He warned us of grizzlies in the area, with their cubs, and that we should avoid them. We told him we had already seen the tracks and asked what we should do about coming upon a bear unexpectedly. His advice was to bang pots and pans while hiking and to give the bears plenty of room. We were so thoroughly cold and soaked to the bone that we thought of asking him for a ride back, but the clouds were lifting, the sun was shining, and suddenly we felt a re-ignition of energy and purpose for being there. We started a fire, ate a hot breakfast, and started the long hike back, banging pots and pans the entire way. How ironic, I thought, not to be able to enjoy the rare and majestic silence that permeates this beautiful place because we have to make this awful noise. The woodland spirits would be happy to see us go.

Our packs, although equipped with hip belts and aluminum tubing, were still heavy as hell. I carried the tent, and my pack weighed at least fifty pounds. To get it on my back required crooking my leg and then swinging the thing onto my knee, twisting my waist to get my arms through the straps, fastening the hip belt, and then feeling how the weight distribution is working once I took a step or two. We sat down for a rest. About forty feet away, I got a good look at a gray fox that had been following us on the trail. Banging on pots and pans was more of an attraction than a warning for this little guy. I guess he liked a parade. When we stopped, he stopped. Then he looked rather curiously at us and started trotting our way. Having the wisdom of a young fool, I freaked out and stood up. I couldn't believe that a wild animal would approach a human if it wasn't rabid. When he got within twenty feet, he stopped, took one look at the upright hairless ape, and took off into the brush. What would have happened if I had just remained calm, like with the bighorn? The fox probably would have come right to our feet, having never seen a human before. Opportunity lost.

The next night was spent in a hotel in downtown Banff. We needed to dry out and get reorganized. Banff catered to a rudimentary type of tourism and there were a few curio shops on the main drag. One place was part curio, part tourist information, and part museum (or at least tried to be). Along with key fobs and so-called Indian artifacts, it had a display of the ubiquitous "Mermaid Child Skeleton." It was a rather small and poor one, fashioned from the remains of what I can only guess would be the cleaned bones of a roadkill opossum, some duck feet for hands, a mounted carp tail, and topped with a rhesus monkey skull. Poor thing; I'm sure it took its revenge, for its Frankensteined state of affairs, upon the dreams of all the little children smearing their noses against the glass case. Later we walked to the end of town and saw the Fairmont Banff Springs Hotel from a distance. This is Canada's premier hotel palace for the rich. I could only afford a postcard of it.

After a good night's sleep, it was time to say goodbye to Banff. We got back onto the Trans-Canada and scoped out a place to wait for a ride west. As we walked onto the road, I noticed there were a lot of other hitchhikers who had the same idea. This was not a good thing. There were maybe half a dozen scraggly guys posted, along with their canvas rucksacks, all along a great curve of road. I wasn't sure at first how many there were because of the curve but one thing I was sure of: there were too many of us. Worst of all, no one was getting rides. I looked at this predicament and thought what if rather than be the *first* hitchhikers, we walk to the end of the line and become the *last* hitchhikers? Could it be possible that a driver, after seeing and passing all these people would have a change of heart and pick up the last hitchhiker... especially a girl and guy? I told Jewell my plan and we started sauntering past all these guys. They kept popping up, one after another as we rounded the curve. Finally, after walking about half a mile, we put in some distance from the last person, like everyone else did between themselves, and waited. Suddenly we saw this short figure coming around the bend, walking straight towards us. He was not scraggly. In fact, he was very well groomed—clean shaven, hair combed, neat as a pin. He was older than us, maybe mid-thirties. He wore a red and white jersey jacket and carried a matching sports bag. Khaki pants, white socks, and shiny black shoes completed his attire. He looked like he was right out of somebody's high school yearbook circa 1955. The smell of cheap aftershave, or a pungent deodorant, filled the air.

"Hulloo," he said.

"Howdy," we replied.

"I noticed you came all the way down here to catch a ride."

"Oh, yeah, gee there're a lot of hitchhikers out today." We shuffled our feet. "I didn't know there were so many till I rounded that curve."

"Oh, so you didn't come down here thinking you might get a ride if you were the last on the line?"

"Oh, no, no," we said. "We had no idea all these people were here, we're just trying to find a spot you know?"

"Ah, well, let me introduce myself," he said. "I am a gentleman of the road. Now, because you are so young, I'm going to let it pass. But there is one thing that you never do and that is BUTT IN LINE! So now you know, don't let it happen again."

Apparently, the end of the line is the front of the line. We had committed the ultimate hitchhiker's sin.

"Oh gee, we're really sorry. We had no idea. Hey man, where you headed anyway?"

"Vancouver," he said over his shoulder and promptly stomped away.

We stayed where we were and got a ride in ten minutes. I had no idea there was such protocol.

The quality of our rides from Banff to Sicamous were scattered and sparse; a ride here, a ride there. My biggest impression of our drivers, who all seemed to be of British descent, was that they were quite naïve about things like natural resources and the environment. The Native Americans and French Canadians we spoke to seemed a little more on the ball. When the Brits learned we were from the States they would gloat that Canada was ahead of the game when it came to conservation of resources, and of how Americans were so wasteful. But at the same time, they liked to talk about how big and long their trains were, with all the cargo moving to and fro across their great land; how big their factories were and look at their wonderful trucking and commerce going on. And all of this is possible because they were so good with their natural resources. I couldn't make sense of this idle "travel talk." It seemed to me that all this activity produced just the opposite—that they were years behind the U.S. in understanding, or even considering, that there might be a problem. If you're gouging into nature with all your free enterprise, you're going to end up like everyone else. There was a right-wing flavor to these people. Another ride, a middle-aged woman with auburn hair and pale blue eyes, said she was against the policies of her government regarding conservation and agreed with my assessment. But then she proceeded to claim that British Columbia's provincial constitution was more or less a replica of something Himmler had established in Germany, circa 1933. I couldn't unscramble what she was talking about. Was she just exaggerating to make a point? Or was she actually crazy? She invited us to her home for tea. Her house was a small gray weather-beaten affair surrounded by flowers and a garden; it was very cozy. We took a rest there for about an hour and had a pleasant time. As we were getting ready to leave, she picked a pint of strawberries for us, along with a few radishes from her garden. We thanked her for the gift and walked back to the road.

Our next ride was from a guy who said he was young too, like about our age. But he was not young. There was something about him that felt like he was still living in the 1960s. I couldn't quite put my finger on it, but everyone who gave us rides in this area, most of them in their forties, had this very simple and anachronistic way about them; more than just old-fashioned, they seemed to be living in another era and were woefully clueless.

By nightfall we had only made it to Sicamous and found no legitimate place to camp, so we made camp on a forest-bearded hill somewhere on the edge of town. The hill lay below the road and was at a 45-degree incline. It was very uncomfortable but the only surreptitious spot we could find. Further down was a flatter area, with tall reeds in a little valley, but I heard dogs barking and saw the lights from some nearby houses, and so thought better of it. We had already been arrested for entering a foreign country with intent to traffic narcotics, why get arrested for vagrancy as well? This would be the first time we'd just flop by the side of the road and hope for the best.

As dawn broke, and with hardly any sleep, we stood with our thumbs out and got a ride halfway to Kamloops. Rides seemed to be disappearing, not that there weren't plenty of cars passing us by. Perhaps the locals were just too conservative here to pick up a couple of tramps. So after standing around for an hour or two, I had an idea to set Jewell up by herself on the road while I lay hidden in the ditch with my pack. It worked. Within a few minutes we had a customer who couldn't resist picking up a female hitchhiker. As soon as he stopped, I hopped out of the ditch with my pack and headed for his station wagon.

"Oh, no room, no room!" he cried.

"Oh, sure there is!" I shot back. The guy had a big empty station wagon for chrissakes. We climbed in and made nice. You always have to do a tap dance for the driver; find a common ground somehow and keep them entertained even if they don't know how to be entertaining. Together you reach a lot of blasé and untrue conclusions about life, and then they feel richer for the experience. Having Jewell there made it easy to banter back and forth and keep the driver engaged. It was an art we were beginning to perfect.

Mr. No Room dropped us off in Kamloops and then we were stuck for five hours. Not that there wasn't a lack of potential rides slipping by. A cavalcade of RVs came rolling past, one after another. It was a ritualized procession of summer vacationers. There were Winnebagos, Beavers, GMCs, Shastas, Golden Falcons and Airstreams. All of them driven by the bloated man with the grinning wife who gazed out upon the funny scarecrow hitchhikers—we were just part of their picaresque and pleasured view.

"My God, can you believe this?" I asked.

"We don't look *that* dangerous do we?" asked Jewell.

I gave her a sardonic smile. "We probably smell worse than we look."

"The only vehicles out here are these RVs," she said.

"Yeah, and there's plenty of room...the pigs." I wished for every clown who passed us by to sit on my barbed hitchhiker's thumb for an eternity. We gave up and hiked into town, looking for a bus.

Gentleman of the Road

The bus wasn't due at the station for another hour so we decided that one of us could walk around town and scope it out while the other stayed with the packs. Jewell was tired so I left her at the station and walked a couple of blocks. I was looking for snacks for our trip into Vancouver and bought some chocolate. I was gone for maybe a half hour before sauntering back to the station when I heard a dim wailing in the distance. I couldn't quite figure out what it was. As I got closer to the station the wailing got louder and then I heard it: *ROLLIE!!!* It was Jewell yelling for all she was worth—duende shooting up out of the earth, up her spine, and manifesting in her vocal cords. I ran as hard as I could—the bus was early! I climbed aboard a bus filled with disgruntled passengers, all waiting for this long-haired idiot to show up. Jewell said the driver was giving it another five minutes and that's all. We could have been stuck in Kamloops for the night.

From Kamloops the terrain became drier. I'm not sure what route we took, but I think we left the Trans-Canada. We were flowing south through Canada's Wild West with its arid mountains and pine freckled hills. The evening bruised the sky as we skipped across Chilliwack and the Fraser Valley. The lights of Vancouver greeted us in the distance, becoming brighter as we rolled from the somnolent darkness into this vibrant city on the coast. Somewhere, somehow, we located a hotel in downtown Vancouver near the waterfront, not far from the bus terminal. We checked in late and slept hard.

The West Coast

In the morning, we walked to a corner restaurant with our backpacks. From our table we could see Vancouver Harbor across the way and were pleased to have finally made it to the coast. I had an oyster omelet. Our waitress saw our packs and wanted to know where we were from and where we were headed.

"The States. It took us sixteen days to get here," I said.

"Have any suggestions for things to see before we head south to California?' Jewell quipped.

"Oh, you should see the aquarium before you go; it's not too far, just down the way in Stanley Park."

"Great!" we said.

"And if you have time, you should check out Vancouver Island."

We had time. Not a lot of money left, but what the heck, maybe we would do just that.

Gentleman of the Road

A bus took us to the aquarium but there were so many people, so many camera-toting tourists, that it quickly became an annoying waste of time. Once again, as we trudged along with our backpacks, I felt like we were being scrutinized in the same condescending manner like those who had passed us by on the road to Kamloops. We took the bus back to where we started and found transportation to the Horseshoe Bay Ferry Terminal. We were headed to Vancouver Island.

It was wonderful to be traveling out on the water, momentarily free from the road and the grasping for rides. We stood at the prow and became human figureheads of the ferry; islands and peninsulas rising up to meet us, swathed in their mists and fogs. We were entering a mystery.

The ferry came to port at Nanaimo. We roamed into town in the late afternoon and found a small hotel with a pub. Rooms were cheap, probably because they were above a pub that could become noisy at night. The habitués were grizzly sailor-fisherman types, hunched over their grog and pretzels. I noticed there were two doors leading into the place, one marked for men and the other for women. So there were two entrances for the sexes, but once they were in, they could mingle. British Columbia had some strange liquor laws. When I inquired about a room I asked the bartender about the separate entrances. He just shrugged and said, "It's the law." Perhaps the doors were monitored for single women who could be profiled as prostitutes. Whatever the reason, once the sun went down the party started. We hardly got any sleep. A pop country singer wailed all night on his twangy electric guitar, getting louder as the liquor warmed, while our room bounced like the inside of a drum.

In the morning we hitched along the eastern coast, via Island Highway E to Parksville. There were stunted palm trees all along the way out of Nanaimo. Canadian palms? Who knew? Somewhere along the way, a driver told us we should check out the Pacific Rim Trail if we liked hiking. It was on the other side of the island and you got there by going through Port Alberni. We headed west through the mountainous center of the island, past beautiful Cameron Lake. Everyone we met on the road was as friendly and helpful as could be; I had never met a happier bunch of people. At Port Alberni we got directions for our final assault to the west coast and got a ride in a logging truck from a driver who was going to Bamfield, a tiny speck on the map just north of the Pacific Rim National Park Reserve. The weather changed suddenly and started to rain, and we were glad to get picked up so quickly. It was a long ride down a very bumpy gravel road—the smell of wet dirt filling the cab as we rode into the shower, the forests getting thicker and greener. He finally let us off at the campground where the Pacific Rim Trail begins. We were looking the grounds over, trying to get our bearings when a skinny man with dirty blonde hair and glasses too big for his face came over and introduced himself.

"Well, howdy. Are you folks friends of Jesus?" he asked.

"Uhm…well…what?" I floundered.

"This is Camp Ross. Are you here for Bible camp?"

"No, we're looking for the Pacific Rim Trail," I said.

"Oh." He looked us up and down. I was not very fond of Evangelicals, with their prescribed agendas, and was starting to dislike this guy.

"Where yuh from?"

"The States."

"Just got a call over the CB to be on the lookout for two runaways; hitchhikers from the States."

I gave him a sour look. We were too old to be runaways. And anyway, we were just too old. Period.

"Yeah, well good luck," I said and started to walk away.

"Wait a minute, the trailhead's over there." He pointed to a clump of bushes at the edge of the trimmed grass. Unable to intimidate us, he changed the subject to his Bible camp, the weather, and the local indigenous tribes he was trying to convert to Christianity.

"What about the Native Americans?" I asked.

"Oh there's a village about thirty kilometers down the Pacific Rim." We walked over to an information board where he pulled out a brochure for us that showed a map of the trail, along with a black and white photo of a gigantic carved head covered in vines. This head was carved from the trunk of a giant redwood that grew in the area. The sculpture was located somewhere near their villages, some of the oldest in North America dating back four hundred years or so.

"Yaas, these Indians are hard to convert. They think their Mother Ocean will provide for them. They claim anything washing up to shore is a gift meant only for them."

I was tired of listening to him and wanted to start the trail. We needed to set up camp before nightfall.

"Well, it starts over there." He pointed again. "But don't eat any shellfish, the Indians claim there's a red tide."

"Okay, thanks for the tip," I said as we marched off.

"Do you really think our parents are looking for us?" Jewell asked.

"That was a load of crap," I said. I couldn't believe she thought such rubbish could be true. I was starting to realize that Jewell had a hypervigilant fear of her father and remembered the time she broke up with me simply because he didn't approve of our relationship. What was he, an omnipotent entity capable of scanning the universe, able to rout us from any and all points on the globe? As much as I admired Jewell's street-smart savvy, I couldn't comprehend the occasional naiveté.

Meanwhile, the trail was glorious—so lush, and so thick with vegetation. I had never seen so many strange kinds of flowers, ferns, mosses, and majestic trees. Some of these cedars are eight hundred years old. It was the first temperate rainforest I'd ever experienced. After a couple of hours, we came upon a lighthouse at Pachena Point and ran into its keeper. He was a young man with a beard, taking a break from his work. He told us there was a nice beach to camp at a little further down the trail. We said it was too bad about the red tide.

"What red tide?" he asked. "It doesn't look red to me!"

"That's what the Indians told the camp director."

"Oh, well," he laughed. "They've been saying that for the last three years. I just think they don't want the whites to be horning in on their turf. You can eat the shellfish."

He went on to say there were bad feelings amongst the natives because of an incident involving the Canadian Army who used the trail for training. The trail crosses a couple of rivers and fording them is a challenge. There was an indigenous ferryman, a Pacheedaht, who for the gift of a case of beer would take you across the Kanawa River in his little boat. But the ferryman wasn't there one day when the army came marching through and so they took his boat, loaded it up with too much weight, and promptly sunk it. Now the ferryman was no longer taking anyone across.

"Well, that's too bad," I said. "We're probably too tired to make it down that far anyway."

We asked him about his job and he said, "You might be interested to know that the Pacific Rim, in these parts, is also known as the 'Graveyard of the Pacific.' There's at least one shipwreck every mile down along this coast. In fact, you'll see an old boiler from a nineteenth century wreck still standing out from that beach I told you about. You'll see it at low tide."

We thanked him and moved on to the beach, finding it in the late afternoon. It was strewn with big logs, washed in from God knows where. We set up the tent and had a lovely evening by the fire, reviewing the day and our food supply.

"Isn't this lovely?" Jewell scanned the beach in the twilight. A thin slice of moon hung over the black and silent forest while the fire bathed us in its flickering glow.

"I could stay here forever," she said.

"I wish we could," I said.

"I'm really feeling great about this trip. I think we'll be fine in California."

"Yeah, I'm so happy to be a million miles away from my parents," I said.

"So you don't think…"

"That your dad knows where the hell we are? Don't be silly, that's ridiculous. Nobody knows where we are. We have disappeared."

"Still, I'm worried about him. I hope he doesn't have a heart attack or something."

"He'll be fine. You worry too much. Anyway, you can always write them when we stop. You'll see."

Beach sand makes for a comfy bed and we slept quite soundly, waves softly shushing through the night.

After breakfast, we relaxed and took a leisurely look around. With all the sun-bleached and barkless logs, there were plenty of places to sit. I pulled out my box of watercolors and painted the beach scene into my journal. Painting a scene ties your memory to that moment much more efficiently than gazing at a photo. Looking at this image now brings me back to that beautiful sunny day: no clouds in an azure sky, a dark phthalo-blue ocean with ochre sand, a touch of cadmium yellow and viridian evergreens standing guard on the shore. I can still smell the crisp salty air with just a hint of pine. Looking at that vast expanse of ocean made me realize that there were degrees to freedom. The freedom one felt on the

94

road was not like the one felt while sitting on the edge of this continent. Traveling for free on the road carried certain stipulations: waiting in limbo for a ride, hoping the driver was not a sociopath, hoping you had enough food, enough money. Of course the payoff was meeting interesting characters and seeing new vistas. But faced with this great emptiness now lying before me I could see a deeper meaning in being free. I was not dependent on anyone; I was not privy to the usual social order. Moreover, the energy released by this infinity of water had a way of displacing your own energy and freeing you from yourself.

It was low tide, and as the lighthouse keeper said, there was a ship's boiler standing out a few hundred feet from shore. Shallow tide pools puddled the basalt that lay beyond the sand. I had never seen sea urchins before, and they were everywhere—along with crabs, starfish, and mussels. I wondered if barnacles were good to eat. I saw these flat, conical things attached to the rocks and decided to try and pry one off. I picked and struggled at it for about twenty minutes, and was about to give up, when suddenly it popped off. I looked down at this poor miserable creature I had just traumatized and felt sorry for it. Even if it was edible, which I later learned it was since it was a limpet, I didn't have the heart to eat it. The muscle that gripped the rock so ardently was twitching like a newborn or an animal in its sleep. I hoped I hadn't permanently destroyed its beautiful little world and tried to stick it back onto the rock. It wouldn't stay, so I dropped it back into the water. Maybe it would heal and crawl back to its brothers and sisters. The mussels, however, were a different story. I showed them no mercy and collected quite a few. We had them for supper and they were delicious.

We used the beach camp for a base and hiked a little further down the trail, but we were too tired to do much more and returned before nightfall. I really wanted to see the totem head covered in vines that was pictured in the brochure; it looked to be about ten feet in diameter. But it was too far away. We stayed there for a couple of days and hiked back on the third day.

At the Bible camp we ran into the director again, who was about to take off in his truck for the other side of the island that afternoon. He had to pick up supplies in Duncan and offered us a ride. He knew the shortcuts—all the unmapped logging roads—hooking up with the Pacific Marine Road that would take us through Lake Cowichan and on to Duncan. We threw our packs onto the truck bed and crowded into the cab. It was a very bumpy ride, much worse than the gravel road we came in on. I was doing okay with this guy until he said, "Gee, I sure would hate to leave you stranded out here—none of these roads are mapped, you know."

I never understood why some drivers did this—tell you it sure would be awful if, or gee, you know what happened to a couple of hitchhikers down this very road two weeks ago? At that point I started memorizing the sequence of his turns onto new roads in case we had to escape and go back to the camp.

Jewell was sitting next to him, and I was at the window. When the road got really bumpy, he said to Jewell, "Hang on! If you need to grab onto my belt loop there, go right ahead!" I think he wanted her to grab on to something else. We finally made it to our destination and were happy to get rid of this guy.

Duncan was a pleasant little town with not much going on. Our traveler's checks were dwindling away but the exchange with the Canadian dollar worked pretty well in our favor. We could afford to splurge six bucks for a room now and then. We found another cheap hotel and reorganized. It was sad to leave the beauty of the Pacific Rim, but the tradeoff is always a nice hot shower when you're back in civilization. The next day we hitched down to Victoria and took a ferry across the Salish Sea to Port Angeles, Washington. Rides were not that great from Duncan to Victoria, and it had taken us all day to get there. We walked down the main drag of town, looking for yet another hotel. We also felt the difference in the people. Americans had their own version of nationalism, expressed in an almost brutish sort of way. The street was filled with American flags as far as the eye could see; huge billboards of Uncle Sam and flag stickers everywhere. There was an Orwellian feel to it all. The woman who ran the hotel was fat, ugly, rude, and gruff. She charged us double for something much worse than what you'd expect to get in Canada. Welcome home.

We caught a ride early the next day down Highway 101, heading for Tumwater just south of Olympia. From there we would catch Interstate 5, which would take us all the way into California. It took two quick rides to get there—one from a karate instructor in a cramped but sporty car who had little cuts and scars all over his head and hands. I guess he broke too many boards. The other was from a guy who liked playing the game of "guess what I do for a living." After examining the karate kid from the previous ride, with all his nicks and scrapes, I started looking at the new guy's hands. They were perfectly clean and very smooth...too smooth. The first thought I had was Mafia. I was afraid to guess. Life, when you're hitchhiking, is very precarious and playing games with strangers is not something you look forward to. I was convinced he was a hitman, a contract killer. There was something about him that was not quite right, something treacherous; a smooth operator. What could look vaguely ominous very often turned out to be just another silly character. I should have known when he told us he was a preacher.

The preacher let us off near the ramp to I-5. We were there for about fifteen minutes when a moving van pulled over. A bald-headed man with a cigar clenched in his teeth looked back at us and shouted from the window, "Hey, you wanna make twenty bucks?" Jewell and I looked at each other.

"Yeah, how?" I shouted back.

"I gotta deliver a piano and need another hand."

"How long will it take?"

"Not more than an hour!"

We decided that Jewell would stay with our gear while I went to help the movers. I wasn't keen on splitting up— anything could happen. But you're always taking a chance on the road and we needed the money.

"Okay!"

It took less than an hour. When I returned, Jewell said, "There were quite a few guys driving by wanting to give me a lift."

"Yeah, I'll bet. Glad you're okay," I said. I was glad for our little fortune and that nothing terrible had happened. In the next instant another car pulled up.

"Where ya headed?"

"California!"

"Hop in!" And we were flowing south, all the way to California on this one ride.

Jay, our driver, was about our age and going to Los Angeles. He was a student at the California Institute of the Arts and said he had John Baldessari, a very important conceptual artist, for a teacher. Jay had short dirty-blonde hair, pale gray eyes, and wore nondescript clothing; there was a coolness about him, nothing flashy. He considered himself an ex-painter and was into conceptual art, as was I—a hot topic for artists then. Like a lot of art students at the time we acknowledged Duchamp and his influence on contemporary trends. Needless to say, we had a great time talking although he did strike me as slightly aloof on the subject of art. The act of painting was considered to be on the chopping block yet I still felt the need to paint. In the art world, painting is continually dead or dying and continually being reborn. That's part of what it is. The king is dead, long live the king.

Interstate 5, the Cascade Wonderland Highway, was a fast and furious shot into California. Jay was exhausted and handed the driving over to me while he took a nap in the back. Jewell and I were very excited to see the "Welcome to California" sign go zipping by. The country seemed infinite and golden, just like we expected. We hadn't gone very far across the border when I noticed a long line of cars up ahead. I couldn't understand why everyone was stopped when obviously a clear lane off to the left was there for the taking. Having the momentum of hundreds of miles behind me, I rushed headlong into the other lane and floored it. I didn't know about these folks but I had places to go. There was no station structure for the California Border Protection Station then—or maybe there was, I don't know, I didn't see one. There were no signs either. All I saw was a very irate border agent in a khaki outfit flagging me down at the end of my run. Jay was startled out of his nap.

"Wait! What are you doing?" Jay asked.

"What do you mean?" I asked.

At the end of the road, a couple agents were waiting for me. I rolled down the window to talk to the nice man.

"Where the hell do you think you're going?" the agent said.

"Uhm, I don't understand—I saw all these cars and couldn't figure out why they had stopped."

"I'm sorry, officer." said Jay from the backseat. "My friend here isn't from California—I've been letting him drive. I was asleep."

The agent explained that you had to declare any agricultural products you might be bringing into the state. It was like crossing into a foreign country.

"Well, I'm really sorry officer. I had no idea." I was afraid we would have to go back into the line that stretched into infinity.

"Hmmph…well…do you have any fruit or vegetables or plants of any sort to declare?" he said.

"No, sir."

"Okay, go ahead then."

He let us go, and we were all rather jubilant. A few more hours of these gently rolling hills and we would be in Berkeley. Somewhere outside of Sacramento, Jay took over the driving. He knew the Bay Area and would drop us off. He went out of his way and I couldn't thank him enough for that. He was a very kind person.

Late afternoon, we came into Berkeley, thanked Jay for a terrific ride and wished him well. We didn't know where we were going or what we would do for the night. Instinctively, we took a bus up University Avenue towards the Berkeley campus and got off to the south of it. We asked some students if they knew of any cheap hotels nearby and someone mentioned a place on Telegraph Avenue, just around the corner. We found it and checked in. It may have been called "The Berkeley Hotel" or "The Hotel Berkeley." I have no idea.

I think it was a brown brick building located at Telegraph and Durant. The clerk at the front desk was from Chicago. The place was a dump—rooms with a bathroom down the hall. We stayed there for a week on the second floor and had forty dollars left.

Berzerkeley

In the morning, I flung open the unscreened window to an arid shock of cobalt sky. The sun in California radiated out and around everyone, showering us with light as we gazed over the rooftops towards the San Francisco Bay.

Telegraph Avenue was one big hustle. Freaks of every color and size were always calling out to you and getting in your face. But you only get hustled if you let yourself get hustled. I didn't expect the "Summer of Love," I knew that was gone, but I didn't expect such a hard-edged nastiness either. I don't know what I was expecting coming to California — maybe nothing, maybe just to see it for what it was. I saw a woman in a flowery mumu, not much older than myself, bleating to the passing crowd, "Doesn't anybody care? Doesn't anybody care?" I don't know what the problem was. It sounded like a sad swan song from a bygone era and nobody cared. I didn't care either.

The street vendors laid out all sorts of junk on dirty sidewalks while Hari Krishnas clanged away on their finger cymbals at the corners. The Krishna people were always giving out free food like ghee rice on paper plates, trying to hook you into a conversation about their religion. I found it interesting that when I was in the Midwest, I couldn't stand the proselytizing of Evangelical Christians. But here I had a lot more tolerance. On the Minneapolis campus they were everywhere, assuming a superior posture and ready to guide your sorry ignorant soul to Jesus. I used to shut them up by blurting, "I don't care how big your dick is, I'm not interested." It was a showstopper. But here there were Christians, Hindus, Muslims, Wiccans, you name it; everybody vibing on something and everything co-existing. I watched a red-haired Irishman, a fiery fellow, preaching hell and damnation to a bemused crowd on the Berkeley campus when a Muslim in a white robe and cap walked up next to him and, facing the crowd, began singing, "God loves you...God *looooooves... yooooouuuu*...He wants you to be *haaaaapyyyyy*..." He sang it in that beautiful minor key; the Islamic call to prayer. The audience grew and everyone was having a good time. Even the Christian, who kept bellowing his hellfire tirade, couldn't keep a smile from drifting across his face. They were both going at it loud and strong, and neither one would give up. I think this incident encapsulates the Cosmic Carnival that was Telegraph Avenue in 1975. Everything was tolerated, and everything was celebrated.

The first thing we needed to do was transfer our money from a bank in Minneapolis to one in Berkeley. We would need as much as possible if we were going to find an apartment, never an easy task. Everything was twice as much as what we were used to. There were some beautifully funky ones in our price range but the cockroaches were rampant; the kitchen cupboards writhed with a thriving bugopolis. We refused to live with them. One landlord, a good ol' boy in a white cowboy hat, was quite adamant that his apartments were clean: no cockroaches. He took us to an apartment that was still inhabited by a Hispanic family. I didn't know if they were getting kicked out or what but it seemed a little weird. When we got there, he said, "Now, I gotta warn ya, the lady still livin' here, she's real nice but she don' speak," he said.

"What do you mean…she doesn't speak?"

He looked at us as if we didn't get it and we didn't. "I mean, she don' speak Anglish."

The door opened and a lovely middle-aged woman greeted us.

"Hola," said Jewell, "¿Como esta?"

"Hola, bien."

"Oh, yer wife speaks Spanish, does she?" he said, quite amazed.

"Yeah, a little…I guess."

Jewell put on a muy grande smile and said, "¿Este apartamento tiene cucarachas?"

"Oh, sí, sí…mucho," she was positively beaming.

"Well, now, ain't that sumpin.' She kin speak it," said our cowboy.

"Muchas gracias," said Jewell, both of them nodding to each other as if they were at a high school reunion.

"Okay, we've seen enough," Jewell said. "I think this apartment might be too small."

"Well, okay, I got s'more openin' up soon—I kin letcha know."

"That would be great," we said.

I whispered to Jewell, "What was *that* all about?"

"I'll tell you later," she whispered. Maybe the lady was trying to hold on to her apartment as long as possible. Or maybe, and more likely, the apartment was infested; maybe both.

We eventually found an apartment that was clean and settled in. It didn't have much soul; dark beige walls and windows that looked out upon other buildings. But it wasn't too far from the campus and it provided a semblance, if only an illusion, of stability that was sorely needed. In reality, we were a hair's breadth from living on the street. There were a lot of people doing just that—tramps, addicts, runaways. I remember rummaging through a clothes box, a hangover from the Diggers era, in the early morning and grabbing someone's toe who was sleeping under the pile. Not a bad place to crash, I thought. After paying out for the apartment, establishing the utilities, and finally getting our money back from Thunder Bay, we had half of our savings left, about four hundred and fifty dollars. The task now was to find work and that would

106

prove to be even harder than finding a place to stay. We signed a one-year lease but would only have a couple of months reprieve before the money ran out. The statewide unemployment rate at this time was around ten percent; the Bay Area seemed a lot higher.

I was depressed as hell and conflicted about working. But the upside for depression is this: you certainly get enough rest. I'd sleep ten hours at a time. Waking up to another stressful day encouraged a hate for reality—all I wanted to do was return to the land of dreams. Here I was, twenty-two years old, no degree and no real experience with anything. A month earlier I was having the time of my life, eating mussels picked from the ocean and exploring a Canadian wilderness, just being free, and now I was supposed to go find work in what would probably turn out to be a factory—not an appealing proposition, but what were my choices? To make matters worse, I was not humble. You can take your damn factory job and shove it. I'm an artist; I don't belong in the machine. I should get paid for doing my own work, not someone else's. And yet, to further complicate matters, I wasn't even sure what kind of an artist I was. I had no product, no studio, and no community. Being an artist was already an alienating experience, but to know absolutely no one and to be living on the fringe like this was a lot more daunting. I constantly doubted even the act of painting. I still had a lot to see and experience before forming any opinions about anything. All I had was a vision of what my life *should* be, not what it was or how to get there. All I knew was that I was dedicated to this thing called art, whatever that may turn out to be. And I mean this in a serious way, not like a painter of landscapes, portraits, or fruit. These modes of illusion glorified technique, and showcased a certain skill, but didn't tell the viewer anything more than what they already knew. It doesn't light up your brain. If you want to see the Renaissance go to a museum but don't confuse it with art. It's art history. A woman once asked De Kooning who of the past he was most influenced by. He replied, "The past does not influence me; I influence it." Even Andrew Wyeth despaired that his fans were more concerned with his technique than his poetic content.

I pictured the true artist's function in contemporary Western culture to be like that of a shaman, someone who could bring forth the latent emotional feelings concealed in everyday life. The artist as shaman is evident in performance art, the "happenings" of the 1960s, and was very ritualistic in nature. The Lakota Indians had "Sacred Clowns," shamans known as *Heyoka*. The Heyoka were contrarians, doing everything in reverse: walking backwards, sitting backwards on a horse, even talking backwards. They brought healing to the tribe through absurdity and satire. I viewed my life as being contrary to society and yet ironically having a place in it as an artist. As a searcher, contrariness was a tool—a litmus test for what is real and what not, what matters and what doesn't. Perhaps the closest translation of this role in Western European tradition would be the court jester in Shakespeare's "King Lear," a character who could satirize the king and get away with it because, through the vehicle of absurdity, the

108

jester told the truth. The king needed his jester the most when he had lost his heart, just as society needs its artists to connect with life's deeper meaning. My card in a Tarot deck would be "The Fool," ready to drop off the cliff of the mundane and have an adventure. And as your friendly local Tarot reader knows, "The Fool" lives next door to "The Magician" card, the shaman.

I applied for work at a couple of libraries—my only work experience from student days—but, not surprisingly, nothing ever came of it. Jewell was just as rudderless. All we had was each other, but I was too despondent to be of much cheer in all of this. I tried to keep my mouth shut about our situation; talking about it wouldn't make it go away. In desperation I wrote a *Letter to the World*. It was a sort of prayer—the flip side of a suicide note. And in some respect it was a defiant reckoning. I just couldn't believe my rotten luck or that the world could just run us over like this. I had too much life left and this is what I tried to convey in the letter. It was addressed to whatever Spirit or Power that was out there. Jewell and I solemnly took it up somewhere into the hillside overlooking Berkeley where I stuck it to a tree. We walked back down through the coarse and yellowed foxtail grass, sat in Ho Chi Minh Park, and just cried.

In Surrealism there is a concept called "objective chance" where the object of one's unconscious desire manifests by coinciding with an unforeseen encounter. This differs from passive serendipity in that it's more of a willed activity. The impetus to do something as irrational as writing a letter to the world was a creative and unconscious act and what followed was a *response* in that, the very next day, we ran into someone Jewell knew. Bob Casey, a fellow she had been friends with in Minneapolis years ago. He came rumbling out of nowhere, directly in front of us on the sidewalk, in his wheelchair. We were just wandering the streets at random—what are the chances of this happening?

"Bob?"

"Jewell? Well, how the heck are you?!"

"Just great! When did you move out here?"

"Couple uh years ago. Who's this?"

He sidled up to me and gave the most beneficent smile. With his red hair, freckles, and pale green eyes he was the living image of Jimmy Olsen, the all-American boy. I felt an immediate sense of relief.

"We hitched out here a couple of weeks ago," began Jewell, "and we're getting kinda desperate for money."

"Where you livin'?"

We told him.

"Get out of that and come stay with me and Eileen—she's my girlfriend. You can stay on my porch if you like and I think I can find you some money too."

We were overjoyed. We would quit our lease and camp out on his porch, while the weather was good, until we got on our feet with jobs. Strangely enough, his house was just across the street from Ho Chi Minh Park where we had spent some tearful moments the previous night.

Gentleman of the Road

We immediately posted a notice on campus for our apartment lease takeover, using Bob's phone number. The rent was really cheap at a hundred and forty per month (about a third the price for a bugless one-bedroom apartment in Berkeley). We had no problem in finding a decent looking, young, hardworking, bright-and-shiny couple to take over. We brought them to our landlady, who also lived in the complex, and sat down, all of us together, for the interview. During the interview she kept wringing her hands and putting on a show of being put out—an elderly woman with too many diamonds on her fingers. She wanted to know where they worked, did they have references, etc., all the while comparing their social stature to our own and the mistakes she had made with "this couple." Jewell and I were being shamed in front of these folks.

Finally, I said, "What the hell do you care? You're getting your money." She was flabbergasted that anyone would speak thusly to her; maybe she had early dementia, I don't know.

Afterwards, as the four of us descended "her majesty's" stairs into the street the guy turned and said, "Yeah, that was weird; what does she care?"

Sleeping on Bob's porch was not all that bad, especially when the weather was so fine. I learned later, when the rains wouldn't come, that we were in a drought. There were a couple of tennis courts over in the park and every morning we'd wake up to the pop-pop-popping of tennis ball volleys. Ho Chi Minh Park was dubbed as such by community activists in 1971 in protest of the Vietnam War. The park's official name,

111

and mostly referred to now, is Willard Park; named after Frances Willard, a suffragette. The politics in Berkeley are so whacky—I had never seen such a conglomeration of wealth and Marxist ideology in one place; armchair Socialists sitting cozily in their beautiful houses on the hillsides. Also dotted around this park, in the late evenings and early mornings, was a caravan of hippie-gypsy wagons—nicely constructed abodes that fit onto the bed of a pickup truck, looking like they came right out of a Tolkien fantasy. I'd watch the inhabitants get up and out every morning to wash their faces and brush their teeth at the public fountains.

I hung out a lot on the campus and spent hours at Moffitt Library. It was an island of refuge. I'd sit near a small stream that ran through campus, reading books I had to sneak out since I wasn't a student (I'd return them). Dragonflies lazily sunned themselves on the leaves of plants I didn't know the names of. I traced the shadows of tree leaves that poured onto my blank journal pages and dated it for posterity: "Shadows of leaves, August 24, 1975, 3:30 pm." Also on campus is the University of California Berkeley Seismological Laboratory where you can view the quivering output of the Hayward Fault that slices through the campus and hills not too far from our sleeping porch.

One good thing, among others, about the Bay Area is how the city limits abruptly stop at the Wildcat Canyon and Tilden parks. You can't build beyond the limit, there's no urban sprawl, and these wilderness areas are so close you can actually walk to them from an urban setting, which was a boon

112

to us since we didn't own a car. Nearby was the Claremont Canyon Regional Preserve, a park filled with eucalyptus trees. It was so dry when we were there that you could smell this turpentine forest and see the dust of dead eucalyptus leaves rise with the heat; tiny motes aglow in the beams of sunlight that lit the forest floor. It was a tinderbox. People we spoke to about this tree said that the Spanish brought it in and that it was a useless weed because the wood twists when it's air dried and is not good for lumber. A little research shows that it was actually brought in by Australians during the Gold Rush. I found it interesting though that Anglo-Americans would typically blame the Spanish. The general vibe I got of California was that it really was a separate country, and that the underlying culture was Spanish. Perhaps the moneyed top layer of this society wanted to blame the underclass.

Bob introduced us to the newly formed Center for Independent Living (CIL) of which he was a member. The CIL is one of the first organizations in the country to advocate for the disabled and offer some political recourse for that community. We could work as part-time attendant care-persons for the disabled through this organization. We immediately signed up for work. It was another waiting game, but eventually, we got assigned to some steady part-time gigs. This suited us perfectly for two reasons: first, it was actually possible, even in Berkeley, to live on part-time work, and second, this type of work fit our manner of living in that, as artist-outcasts, we didn't have to show up at an office or appear to fit in. We would have time for our art. Of course food could not be had without food stamps—something I was accustomed to from student days.

Jewell worked for a woman who had polio when she was a child and so her hands never grew and were very small. She liked to crochet and I think that, due to the size of her hands, she made the most intricate and beautiful pieces. As for myself, I ended up as a care-person for a guy who was politically active and responsible for the ramps you see on all the corners of the streets in Berkeley.

The weather cooled and the money slowly trickled in. Bob offered us a spare bed in the front room of his duplex; we moved from the summer porch to the autumn bedroom. The plan, originally, was that his neighbor would vacate his side of the duplex, whereupon we would then move in and become full-time attendant care-persons for Bob. It didn't happen. But we were quite grateful for the temporary shelter of the room and the use of a kitchen. We had an address now and could write letters to family and friends, letting them know we were okay. Jewell wrote to her mother and was very happy to get a response. She called her mom that night and got an earful concerning my hysterical mother. Apparently, she had launched into a tirade against Harriet over the phone, blaming Jewell for leading her son astray (we had given each set of parents the other's phone numbers, a bad idea in hindsight). But my mother was less shocked about my leaving as she was about Jewell and me "living in sin." Harriet said she could now understand why I had always made such disparaging remarks about my mother. She thought she was certifiable. Thank God I was far away from them.

Sometimes Bob and Eileen would take off for long weekends and we'd have the run of the house. There was something very evocative about the place. It was old, had bare wooden floors, to better facilitate his wheelchair, and was filled with old furniture. An antique Victrola record player lived in the front room. We'd wind it up and play Bob's 78s in the evenings, amused by the cheery Tin Pan Alley from a bygone era. I would often get very nostalgic sitting in their kitchen. I don't know if it was because a kitchen can be the center of a household, like it was at my grandmother's, or if it was the light that filled it. This California light, for me, was primordial. I was quite at peace with it. It was the light of the desert, and it could spark some very early memories of my life in Moab.

One of the strangest memories I had was of communicating with a lizard. I was just beginning to talk then. We didn't speak to each other in sounds but rather in colors. Squares of colors, mostly red and yellow, were shared between us. I felt a communion with this creature. So was this communication or was I just a baby getting dizzy from the heat and dehydration? I heard my parents calling me, the spell was broken, and I had to leave my lizard friend behind. I walked into the sun with them, our long shadows streaming across a landscape that looked like Mars. I've read that a baby's brain has twice as many neurons as an adult, even though an infant's brain is half the size. Synaptic pruning takes place as the child ages, tossing out connections that are weak or not used. Presumably these connections disappear because they offer no use for the child's adaptation to language, socialization, etc. But is it possible that psychedelics reopen these channels? That they don't disappear but merely wake up? I don't know, but I never talked to lizards again.

I also remembered the house where we lived in Moab; a mid-century modern with simple lines and a picture window. I had vague memories of George that were not kindled from the photos my mother showed me—like walking down a hall and seeing him at a desk doing something, maybe paying bills, and the distinct aroma of a cigar. I was still in diapers. I remembered a cold strip of rushing water in our backyard that was about a foot deep, an irrigation ditch that could quickly cool you down in the summer; and a monster road grader that would roar down our graveled street, kicking up a yellow-gray dust. I tasted dirt in that backyard just to see what it was like.

I used to sit on my dad's lap and steer the Jeep while he drove us across rocky flats in various shades of blood orange and ocher. A cool wet canvas bag filled with water lay in the back of the Jeep. He introduced me to echoes that magically inhabited remote canyon walls. Spirits lingered there.

I even remembered getting tipsy once when I was probably around three from my mother's Grasshoppers that were sipped at some neon lighted lounge. After swerving around greasily on a drunken midnight road, we came to the muddy banks of a river, got out, and took a stroll under the stars. I was running into the mud and sinking up to my knees in the cool soft muck. The starry firmament blazed above and almost seemed to be speaking to me, as if I had an intimate connection to these stars, but I couldn't quite grasp what they said. Perhaps it was just a confirmation like, "*Well, here you are*." I twirled in the mud and felt so happy—a drunken three-year-old. On the way home I threw up in the backseat of the car.

So the light in California, by virtue of its catalytic ability to pull up these long forgotten memories, really made me feel like a whole person. I wasn't just some kid that was tossed into Davenport, whose life didn't begin until Bert and Elroy's marriage. I had the start of my existence in this sacred light. I wondered about George, what was he like, and was he even still alive? But I was so immured in the junk of my mother's reality that the thought of looking him up did not even occur to me. If I tried to find him, and succeeded, it would probably kill her. But how would I do it anyway? I'd be looking for a needle in a haystack.

Richmond

Bob lent us his van so we were able to cruise around the area in search of an apartment. By October we had found a nice place, within our budget, in a three-story apartment complex in Richmond. Richmond is one of the cities furthest north in the Bay area—El Cerrito, Albany, and Berkeley to the south, all of them sewn together by the thread of the newly opened Bay Area Rapid Transit (BART); the first fully automated commuter train in the country. We'd ride the BART to work into Berkeley every day.

The apartment was full of light, the opposite of the first place we had in Berkeley. And there was a cozy, familiar odor to it; a lived-in smell from the accumulation of all the other tenants' cooking. In the apartment below lived an ex-hobo and his wife. He was an old Black man who rode the rails during the Depression. I wanted to talk to him about his experiences but he rarely went out and his wife was very protective. I respected his space.

The only furniture we had was a broken chair, an unbroken chair, and a table—all found on the street. The broken chair, missing its back, supported the black-and-white TV purchased from the local St. Vincent de Paul, where we also purchased kitchen utensils and other minor household items. Once the television started to heat up it would go bad with horizontal lines and you had to turn it off. Our bed was on wheels and slid into the wall, rolling beneath the elevated bathroom. The wall-to-wall carpet was suffered with fleas during "flea season," which happened in the fall. There was no getting rid of them but at least they weren't cockroaches. Once their season was over, they would magically disappear. From our second story window you could see rows and rows of houses made of ticky-tacky, as the song goes. Our fat neighbor across the street liked to go fetch his morning paper at the end of his walk wearing nothing but a robe—that he never bothered to tie. He'd dangle along like a pink elephant in drapes. Later we got a cat from a student in Berkeley and named him Busby after Busby Berkeley, the corny film director of the 1930s. Although we didn't have much, we were happy for what we had: an apartment, jobs, and the semblance of a secure future. We could make it here.

The crime rate in Richmond was bad but, where we were, we saw no problems. The downtown area, however, was another story. The Iron Triangle was literally on "the other side of the tracks" from us, and is where most of the crime happened. Going over there to Social Services for food stamps was always a bit dicey with lots of boarded up buildings and nasty vibes; you never felt safe. A recession was going on in 1975 and I'm sure the unemployment rate in Richmond was double the national average. Our social worker asked us questions about ourselves, how we came to the area, and what our plans were. Since we were new in town, and still a bit footloose, he'd ask if we had any plans of going back home. I think he wanted a "yes" for an answer since the system was overloaded and the last thing he needed was a couple of kids from the Midwest.

The Richmond Art Center liked to boast that they were the first museum to exhibit, or perhaps they were even the "home" of, conceptual art. Not sure how true that is but I did enjoy seeing Tom Holland's work while I was there. Like a lot of contemporary art in California, his abstract paintings are fun and celebrate light. There was a neo-Orphist sensibility about them. I also thought his use of untraditional materials was interesting: fiberglass, aluminum, and epoxy paint. Now that we had a base, and a bit of financial security, I felt free enough to explore galleries and museums over in San Francisco. In the museums I saw some powerful Clyfford Still paintings and the work of William T. Wiley. In the galleries, photorealism was in vogue. It reminded me of pop art in a way but not as confrontational, not as Dada. My takeaway from that genre was in its focus on banal subject matter and that it didn't matter what you paint, just do it well. This realization helped to open me up in terms of subject matter; I could start anywhere, just make it work within the arena of the canvas. I carry this conviction to this day. I also went quite often to the Berkeley Art Museum on campus. It boasted a collection of nearly fifty Hans Hoffman paintings on permanent exhibit. Next door was the Pacific Film Archive, housed within the same building, where I watched many underground and avant-garde films. Across the bay was the California Academy of Sciences where we attended a reading by the poet, Josephine Miles.

So all this West Coast cultural stuff was great—I was opening up, settling in, and glad to be in California. I started painting again in our light-filled apartment. I didn't have much money, so I used cheap hardware store paint and large hunks of paper garbage that blew around in the street. I'd collage these papers together and paint on them, letting some of the words of advertisement show through via chance encounters with other elements in the work. There was a lot of garbage—or should I say found objects—in the streets of Richmond, so why not use it? If Tom Holland could make paintings out of industrial material, I could certainly fabricate something from society's waste. It doesn't matter what your material is, just use it well. I eventually managed to scrape enough money together to make one large painting on canvas, using tubes of acrylic paint purchased from an actual art supply store.

I made an "endless drawing" by taking a sheet of paper, composing a non-representational abstraction with pencil and eraser, and then photographing the results at various points in time predetermined by chance operations. The idea was to focus on process, not a finished product, and document the activity; the drawing being disposed of after the activity and documentation. I also took a camera with me to San Francisco, while visiting galleries, and took random shots of the streets following the same chance-determined points in time. Later, I would look for anything interesting in them that might suggest hidden images for possible use in a painting. These activities were my only foray into conceptual art.

Video art was beginning to pop up here and there in San Francisco and I thought I might like to try that as well. When I was a student in Duluth, I had access to a video camera and monitor and staged a performance in one of the campus' many halls. This performance consisted of lying down inside a large cardboard box with the top covered, installing a light source inside, holding a camera on my chest and slowly focusing on the box's interior wall beyond my feet. I slowly panned the horizontals, corners, and verticals, letting the camera move up and down on my chest as I breathed (influenced by Vito Acconci's body-art). I did this for a couple of hours with a large monitor documenting the activity in real time on the outside of the box. I also laid a ring of weather-beaten branches around this "coffin" and monitor that I had gathered from Lake Superior's shore for a ritualistic effect; again, the idea of artist-as-shaman. It was an interesting experiment, but we were so poor, where would I find resources for the equipment? Jewell was also struggling with her art, her writing. Like myself, she was more interested in avant-garde sorts of things and tried

122

her hand at concrete poetry; words being repeated over and over in a Gertrude Stein sort of way. Artists are searchers.

I was still reading through the entire text of the *I Ching* and decided to try asking it a question about itself, much like what Carl Jung does in the forward of this book. Being in solidarity with Jewell's feminism, it always bugged me how chauvinistic the *I Ching* could be at times. So the question I concentrated on asking it was, "why is the *I Ching* often putting women down," or something like that. I took up three pennies, shook them in my cupped hands, tossed them on the table, and counted up their value: two for tails, three for heads. I did this for all six lines, keeping this question of chauvinism in the forefront of my thoughts. The hexagram received was 61: Chung/Fu, Inner Truth. It basically said that if someone needs to judge the actions of men, then the superior man tries to come to an understanding of circumstances that led those people to their decisions. One must know how to pardon. I had to laugh—I was being admonished for not having a sympathetic appreciation, nor an understanding, of how to pardon the book. My interpretation was that times were different then, and that the men who put the *I Ching* together worked with what they had and should be forgiven their shortfalls.

We still managed to keep our thumb in the hitchhiking game while we were living in Richmond—how else do you get around without a car? We'd go camping on the weekends, just to get out of the urban drama. Point Reyes was a destination, across the bay, where there was a place to camp on the beach. We'd build a fire and watch the sunset over the Pacific. It was otherworldly and hard to believe all this natural beauty could be so close to San Francisco.

Jewell learned from her mother's letters that she had an aunt living along the coast, not too far from us.

"Why don't we go and visit her?" Jewell said. "She lives in Bodega Bay, only sixty miles from here."

"Sure, why not. Who is she?"

"Aunt Flo. I don't think anyone in the family has seen her for years."

We hitched out to her home and stayed for the weekend. Aunt Flo lived on the opposite side of a desolate hill where the town was nestled along the coast. She was tall and thin with brown hair and eyes and was constantly in pain—her doctors unable to pinpoint the cause. Perhaps it was from working most of her life as a waitress at a nearby café. Bodega Bay, as everyone remembers, is the setting for Hitchcock's *The Birds*. She was happy to connect with kin and drove us around like the tourists that we were. She took us to the Potter School where the schoolyard scene was shot. At home, her mantle displayed a couple of duck decoys that were used in the movie. The house she rented was very small with no heat in the spare bedroom where we stayed and nearly froze to death. The countryside reminded me of pictures of Ireland or an Andrew Wyeth watercolor—beautiful barren hills with grazing sheep. The night exposed an unfettered sky, encrusted with stars, and the dark silence conspired to shrink space in such a way that the sounds you'd hear at a great distance seemed to be at your very doorstep. Sheep's bells comingling with the nattering of a brook created an assemblage of sounds so eerie and strange that, at first, you're not quite sure what or where it's coming from; a disorienting music coming from the black rectangle of an open door.

Hitchhiking around the Bay Area was a bit more alarming than what we were used to going across Canada. People had real agendas here: oddballs and other nonconformists, usually harmless, but occasionally you'd get a sociopath. One of our rides back from Bodega Bay was with a somewhat raw individual who had a lot to say about society and of his individual perils. He said he had been in and out of prison because of his "honesty" and "calling a liar a liar." He believed in an eye for an eye; tooth for tooth, etc. And don't we agree? "Yeah, sure," I said. I think he trusted me because we were both long hairs. "Right on bro." But Jewell and I were so unnerved by this guy that neither one of us could retain much of what was being said—we just wanted to reach our destination. It occurred to me he was crazy. When he finally let us out of his truck, he gave me a chunk of ginseng for the road. I started chewing it and was quite surprised at the rush; bright as a cup of coffee. I have never had ginseng of that quality since.

We were a little shaken from this experience. When we got back home, I threw off my backpack and sat on the floor of our bare apartment—feeling safe, but positively exhausted.

"That one ride was kind of scary," said Jewell.

"I know. I didn't know where he was going with his tirade."

"Did he really have a beef or was he just crazy?"

"Both."

"It's funny how you can get pulled into a conversation with a stranger and not know how the hell you got there or where it's going."

"You start wondering if you've said the right thing—I couldn't track him, he was talking nonsense at one point. It was amazing he could even drive."

"He kept veering into the oncoming lane whenever he got excited."

"I saw that. Good thing we were in the country."

"I tried to keep it simple—what year his truck was, how long he lived out there," Jewell said.

"Yeah, you did good."

I wrote for the first time to my family, specifically my grandmother, the only person that I missed. I think seeing some of Jewell's extended family, and surviving a questionable ride, encouraged me to write her. I was delighted at her quick response. Of course she was happy that we had found jobs, and that we were settling into a new life, but her reprimand of not telling my parents that I was taking off was a bit disconcerting. She wanted me to write them but I just couldn't. I was not going back into the family drama any time soon.

Dawn, whom we'd left on that forgotten Minneapolis street a year ago, paid us a visit. She'd ditched her dog and hitchhiked with her roommate, Mary, across Canada—the same as us. They parted in San Francisco as Mary was headed for a nanny job down in Santa Maria; she took a bus. It was great to see Dawn again, to talk of old times and reacquaint ourselves with that Midwestern sensibility. We'd felt like aliens for almost a year, living out here on the coast. I liked California for the culture and the natural beauty but we had a hard time making friends. We didn't know where the artists lived, hadn't met any, and felt isolated. We were still working part-time jobs and not really ensconced in a social network that can result from full-time situations, an obvious downside to our freedom. Dawn stayed with us for a few days and then returned to Vancouver. She had a serious romantic interest there—someone she'd met on the road who had given her a ride. Marriage was a looming possibility for her.

In April, Jewell's mother Harriet came to visit us. Again, it was wonderful to see a familiar face. We learned from her that Jewell's father could not bring himself to talk to his wayward daughter for taking off like she did. And he didn't approve of her living with a man without being married. Fritz wasn't a Christian Fundamentalist or anything, that's just the way most parents of our generation were; rules and regulations superseding love. Of course, this type of thing still goes on since people don't really know how or what to think, they only know how to react. Harriet was the only one who could step outside the idiocy of convention, or the biblical straitjacket, because she loved her daughter. She had rented a car and took us out for a fun weekend to Lake Tahoe. Jewell was overjoyed seeing her mother again and I could tell something was beginning to turn in her mind but I couldn't tell what. She was a lot more relaxed when her mother was here. Our life on the road and the continued estrangement that we felt living on the coast was beginning to eat at her. After Harriet left, Jewell started to hate our life in California. Perhaps she missed whatever it was about that Minnesota persona that her mother and Dawn had. Or maybe she was tired of the constant striving that daily life brings to the poor in an urban setting. We started fighting again.

"I can't stand living here anymore. I want to go back on the road," Jewell said.

My heart sunk. "You're kidding. We haven't even been here a year."

"What does it matter? We'll never get ahead here."

"Well, why not? You want to throw everything away and just start over?"

"What's there to throw away?! We have nothing!!"

"We have a decent apartm…"

"Fuck this place! We have an *empty* apartment. We have no money, we have no friends…"

"We have Bob and Eileen…and the guy down the hall that plays the banjo…"

"I need community. I miss my sisters from the women's group. You might be happy as a clam here in your ivory tower art studio, or whatever, but I can't do isolation."

"Fuck off! I don't live in an ivory tower…and I have feelings too, asshole!"

128

A deafening silence ensued. Then, "You can do what you want but it's time for me to go. I'll hitch out of here by myself; I can't stand it anymore."

My head was spinning. I hated the thought of going back on the road, and returning to Minnesota was not an option for me. I didn't like the thought of breaking up. And if Jewell was so adamant about going on the road again I didn't think it a good idea for her to travel alone. I left the apartment and walked around the neighborhood for an hour or more. Like any death, it took a while to process. But in the end, it simply boiled down to sticking with your mate through thick and thin, us against the world. I walked back, resolved and cooled off.

"Okay, maybe you're right," I said. "It's true, we have no ties here; nothing to hold us. But I'm not going home...I'm not going back to Minnesota."

"Okay, that's fair. Maybe if we just get out of this city, you know, someplace nice in the country. We'll find it, I know it, if we just get out of here."

I wasn't sure how we were supposed to make a living in the country if we'd had a hard enough time trying to find work in the city. I was also a bit confused at Jewell's new attitude about urban living since, when we were students, she was of the opinion that living in the city held more opportunities than living in the country. Maybe she just missed the Twin Cities. At any rate, it would soon be time to haul the backpacks out of the closet—we were headed for round two. Our stay in California was less than a year.

Drifters

Once again it was time to close up shop. For me, there was no mirth in this exodus from a hard-earned place in the California sun. Our furniture was lean—simply thrown back to the street from whence it came. The cat needed a home so we advertised with a post on the Berkeley campus. On the day before our departure, I carried him through the BART in a daypack with his head sticking out. Poor Busby was so overstimulated that he became limp as a dishrag. He had no idea the world was so large. His new mom had been frying chicken before coming to pick him up and he was quite interested in her fingers. Busby returned to the place of his birth and went to a good home. We also brought along the bedeviled TV and sold it on the street like any other ragged crook. A guy came out of his nice house and wanted to buy it.

"Does it work?" he said.

"Sure, it works."

"Mind if I plug it in?"

130

"Sure, go ahead."

He plugged it in, voila it worked, and he gave us our twenty dollars. I don't know how or why but, a few minutes later, we ended up walking past his house again to get to the BART station and could hear him yelling and cursing at the goddamn thing from his open door. I'm not proud of this...but we did giggle. The TV taught you that it's not good to watch so much television. It's better to read a book.

We had to return to Richmond and start packing; we'd be leaving the next morning. Again, the two books I would bring were the *I Ching* and my journal. I hadn't used the *I Ching* much on the first trip since there was never a need, we knew our destination, but now we were really going to be using it since our navigation would be no better than a spin of the bottle.

The next morning, we rode the BART all the way to Daly City and then it was a short walk to an entrance ramp through the most god-awful spaghetti of steel and concrete you could ever imagine. The noise was deafening and it felt like we were about to go over Niagara Falls in a barrel. We caught a ride and danced our way through this chaos, managing to hit State Route 1, the great Pacific Coast Highway that hugs this country's western shore. It was Jewell's idea to head south on it after talking to Dawn, who gave us Mary's phone number and address in Santa Maria. Mary said it was okay for us to stay a few days with her and figure out a plan. Our immediate goal was to reach Santa Maria where she had settled into her governess duties with a wealthy man and his two kids. He was a Coors distributor. Dawn said she would fly down with her partner and join us there later. Other than that, we didn't have much of a plan; the general idea was to just get away from urban living and try to find a more peaceful place to live, wherever that may be.

After the tumult of Daly City, we entered a much slower and quieter location. This is where I first noticed the messages that fellow hitchhikers leave on the backs of road signs, often telling you how long you may expect to be standing there. This one read: "from San Francisco to LA the slow way." And it was signed…Frank Zappa. Could it have been *the* Frank Zappa? Was it an old message from, say, ten years ago when he was just beginning his career? Was it a joke? How many Frank Zappas do you suppose there are in California…thousands or just hundreds? Anyway, it made me smile and I took it as a good omen.

We got picked up by some hippies in a blue van. The doors slid open and we threw our packs in—nowhere to sit, as usual, so you toss about like rocks in a tumbler at every turn. Our benefactors were quite jovial as they talked about a couple of hitchhikers who, just last week, were found with their throats cut and left in a ditch by the side of this very road. I hated it when drivers talked like this—not a good way to break the ice. Later we hit the scenic part of the trip and they fired up a joint with Grateful Dead on the 8-track. We toked up to be sociable but I took it in shallow breaths, not wanting to get more paranoid than I already was from the slashed hitchhikers story. I was mildly buzzed, seated on the floor and straining my neck to see the glorious coastline through the van window. We slid through Monterey, home to one of the largest and seminal of rock festivals. The Monterey Pop Festival introduced Hendrix, the Who, Janis Joplin, Otis Redding and countless others to mainstream America. I wished I could have been there but I missed it by nine years.

They left us at Santa Cruz where we caught a ride from a middle-aged guy who was a buyer for a grocery chain. He drove us through Castroville, the artichoke capital of the country. Passing a small restaurant in the shape of an artichoke, I wondered if that's all they served there. We also passed truckloads of broccoli; large green bunches dropping off and rolling across the road. What a waste. I would have gladly scooped them up. Our driver had samples of produce in the backseat and offered us a cantaloupe when we reached the end of our ride. We were very grateful and would have it for breakfast. The last ride for the day dropped us off somewhere around Big Sur where we flopped into a big field by the side of the road. We had landed in a patch of dill, and you could smell it everywhere. The weather was fine, and we didn't need the tent. We were tired as hell. Ironically, our food cache was low. After seeing a piece of America's breadbasket, all we had for supper that night were two bites of cheese, two slices of bread and a carrot. I saved one boiled egg, and of course, the melon for breakfast. We had made it to Big Sur in one day. My mood that night was very solemn—something told me this would not be an easy passage. For my part, it was a reluctant adventure. We had no real destination. But it was also very beautiful there, and here we were watching the evening settle over the Pacific. The setting sun, hovering above its long red reflection, made a dotted "i" on the serene ocean before us. Clouds drifted across in a contrapuntal dance and an eerily gnarled tree in the foreground completed this romantic vision. Later, we were drenched in the ghostly white chalk of a full moon. There was not a soul around.

We were up at first light, ate the melon and the egg, and stumbled to our wayward posts by the side of the road. We caught a good ride all the way down to San Luis Obispo. Our driver was a very chatty woman who pointed out the Hearst Castle in the distance at San Simeon. I'm afraid we were too exhausted to be very cheery for our driver. Thankfully, it only took two more rides from San Luis Obispo and we were at the beer distributor's doorstep in Santa Maria.

Mary answered the door and showed us around. It was a new and very modest house lined up on a cul-de-sac with other expensive-looking homes. Just a mile down the road was the motel where migrant workers and their families lived; dozens of adults piled into tiny rooms.

We were introduced to Mary's employer and his two children: a boy and a girl around eight or nine years old. The house was well kept and quite spotless. One could even say that it was rather sterile; no pictures on the white walls and a grand piano no one played. The children were extremely well behaved—too much so. Other kids in the neighborhood would come over and formally ask if so-and-so could come out and play. These rich kids were unbelievable; no screaming, no

134

running around. They were like little adults, and I could sense they didn't like us. We were shown to the guest room and proceeded to rearrange our gear when I noticed several large gray spiders scurrying out of our packs. We must have picked them up in the dill field at Big Sur. We infected the house.

It was nice to stay in a comfortable place for a few days and get our bearings. Dawn called and had changed plans: she and her boyfriend would be driving down instead of flying and it would be a number of days before they reached us. Sitting up in bed that night, I pulled out an atlas and started flipping pages. What's Upstate New York like? It all seemed so ridiculous; where do you go? Like they say, if you don't know where you're going, any road will take you there. Or as Gertrude Stein had said, "There is no there there." There is anywhere and everywhere. We had become drifters, with no desired destination. Maybe all you do is…go…

Jewell turned to me and said, "So what are your thoughts? Stay on the West Coast or head back East?"

I couldn't believe she would even consider hanging around. What was her point?

"I don't want to just start all over again out here," I said. Los Angeles, just three hours away, looked depressing and strange on television—images of the filthy rich in contrast to the filthy poor, all living in a sprawling metropolis. The poor were stuck out here in cities that had the worst pollution and heat in the nation with no way to escape. I didn't really want to leave the Bay Area to begin with but if we were going on the road we may just as well keep going. The coast was over-subscribed.

"Hell, we've seen the West. Let's go see the East," I said.

We stayed for a couple of days at the house but knew we were wearing out our welcome. We didn't want trouble for Mary. I mentioned to her that her boss seemed pretty aloof and conservative; super straight and very uptight. She laughed and showed us his stash—an ounce of pot tucked under his hat on a top shelf of his closet. "He's a real hypocrite," she said. I guess you have to maintain an image if you're going to do business.

We decided to set up camp and rest for a couple of weeks at Los Padres National Forest, no more than twenty miles away, before starting our journey. I'm not sure why we dawdled, perhaps for the same reason a high diver takes a moment to purvey his leap—just getting up the nerve. After doing some major grocery shopping, Mary dropped us off at the nearest camp. It was very dry and dusty. Dawn was still on the road and would come out to visit us once she got into town.

Being once again rudderless, I pulled out the *I Ching* and asked: *How should we know where and when to stop?* A tossing of the coins produced *Chun / Difficulty at the Beginning*. How apropos. The hexagram revealed that when it is your fate to undertake new beginnings, and all is in the dark, unformed, one must hold back to avert any premature move that could bring disaster. Also, that one needs helpers to overcome the chaos. Great. Well, we've been "holding back" here for a few

136

days now trying to decide what direction to take. I guess the "helpers" were Dawn and Mary—but the extent of their help was only emotional support (which is a lot actually). Maybe other helpers would be good rides. A further reading of Chun mentions that one must put some order into this chaotic beginning like sorting out "silk threads from a knotted tangle" and binding them "into skeins," one must "be able to both separate and to unite." I got stuck on this separate and unite stuff so I asked a further question: *How does one both separate and unite*? The answer was *Chieh/Limitation*. One must have limitations and be frugal, but not be so self-limiting as to cause permanent damage via hardship to oneself or others. In other words, don't become a hobo—get this traveling done with, and settle down somewhere. This hexagram changed in the fifth line to: *Lin/Approach*. It basically talked of success in the spring (we started out this time in May, 1976). But any endeavors after that would bring misfortune. Again, let's get it done. I couldn't get over the *I Ching*. There was always something personal and timely in its advice that was uncanny; always direct and to the point. It was also a comfort in times where little comfort could be found. Of course, the message from an *I Ching* hexagram wasn't always so transparent either. Looking back on a throw of the coins, months later, you might see what it was all about and concur that perhaps you weren't concentrating on the right question. Answers seemed pertinent to what your subconscious already knew, or was really asking; your conscious mind unable to see, or unable to formulate, the right question for the problem at hand.

We were planning on staying for a couple of weeks and exploring the beautiful landscape—we only stayed for one. Dawn drove out to our camp, without her boyfriend, and stayed with us for a couple of days. In the middle of the night, on the last night of her stay, we were awakened by the sound of car wheels abruptly stopping on the gravel, a rowdy couple getting out, and an argument of some sort beginning to foment. A young male voice seemed to be taking command of the situation when, all of a sudden, we heard a loud slap and the distinct sound of a body hitting the ground. The cries and moans of drunken individuals intertwined with accusations and denials and then, *whack*, a body hit the ground again. The three of us looked at each other—our collective stomachs churning. We were still half-asleep, trying to gather our wits, and nerve, to go out there and put a stop to it. This was a primitive camp, so there were no park rangers or even a telephone nearby, which was why the prick chose this place to beat up his girlfriend. We weren't even sure how many were involved—it sounded like more than just two. Suddenly, a fellow camper from across the campsite bellowed, "Get the hell out of here! Families are camping here!" The party got back into the car and sped off into their miserable fucked-up night. Sleep was hard to come by after that. What, if anything, did it portend for our trip? Hitchhiking in Canada seemed so civilized with its public hitchhiking shelters, but I was afraid the States would be a different story.

When Dawn left in the morning, she told us that Mary would bring us some groceries on such-and-such day, but she didn't show on the designated day and, once again, we were getting desperate. I think this was the impetus for our departure—it's good to have control over your food supply as best you can. Like fledglings, we just had to drop out of the nest and hope for the best. We took down the tent and tried our best to shake the dust out of it. The dust was so fine in the campground that it blew through the mosquito netting, making a fine powder on the tent floor. Even the camp water supply, a pipe with a tap stuck into the hard ochre ground, had a viscosity to it like milk. We were drinking dirt tea.

After breakfast we bundled up our gear and headed out to the Cuyama highway, going east. Our rides took us through multiple twists and turns but eventually we made it to Bakersfield; it was hot as hell in the noonday sun. Now I knew why they called it Bakersfield—we were baking. Gone were the dry but cooler San Rafael Mountains. We were now looking at the lowlands. Bakersfield was a dusty cowboy town and the last real outpost on the edge of a vast desert. I was very concerned about that. I hadn't really experienced a desert in my adult life and did not know what to expect in terms of traversing it. Thoughts of getting stuck in the middle of nowhere did not appeal to me. The desert is the only place where I've felt sunlight "raining" with an unexpected weight of light that ceaselessly beats down upon your exposed head. It was quite palpable. In an odd sort of way, the great expanse of the desert felt claustrophobic, as if it were a gigantic room. It was brutal, scary, and unreal.

We decided to make Las Vegas our destination, and to not take any rides that were only going halfway. We lucked out, and by the end of the day caught our desired ride, or rather, our desired destination ride. Within the first hour my usual jovial sense of keeping the driver entertained did not seem to be working. I started feeling uneasy about the guy. We had experienced several questionable rides in our journey but nothing quite as dark as this individual. There wasn't anything in particular that you could point to, it was just a feeling. Perhaps it was the wry smile he perpetually had; a smile that betrayed a peculiar emptiness. Our conversations were short. Jewell and I would look askance at each other…but what could you do? Just try to keep it simple and act naive.

At Barstow we headed north on the Mojave Freeway. The sun had gone down in a fiery blaze a long time ago. The desert was cool now with a full moon presiding over the sun's extinguished kingdom. Gone was the claustrophobia of day as the moon unfolded the desert's true infinity. A shadowy vagueness of forms whipped past the windows of our speeding car whose headlights probed the future like the tails of twin comets.

"It's a real good thing I picked you up when I did." His voice shattered the silent stupor we were drifting into. "I'd sure hate to be stuck out there in that." I looked over at him, and for an instant, that second sight you get when you're on the road kicked in. I saw a skeleton driving the car. You can call it a hallucination but an unconscious image that graces your waking life, without the help of drugs, is a gift and has a truth behind it. My rational mind quickly took over and blamed the long shadows cast by the full moon, mixed with dashboard lights, for the illusion. But I also heeded the warning. I would not drift off again.

We had just crossed over into Nevada when he said, "Looks like we're getting low on gas." I offered him some money. "Nope, won't be necessary," he smiled. He pulled up to an obscure little casino in the middle of nowhere and disappeared into the premises.

For the first time in hours, I stretched out and turned towards Jewell who was in the back seat. "What do you think of this guy?"

"He's creepy."

"Yeah, I know. What do you suppose he's doing in there?"

"Who the hell knows? Maybe somebody owes him money."

"How did he know to stop here? Or did he know to stop here...why here? Where...here..."

Finally, after about an hour, he came back to the car.

"Got gas money," he smiled.

"Oh, yeah?"

"Yeah...blackjack."

Apparently, our driver was very good at blackjack. We were cruising across the Mojave with a skeleton who relied on chance to make it to his destination—not unlike ourselves with the *I Ching*, albeit in a more pragmatic fashion. So he was a gambler—maybe that's what unnerved me. He held his poker

141

face to the world at all times, fastened with a crocodile smile. We were gamblers too.

The night's enchantment eroded into the twilight of dawn as we spotted the carnival lights of Las Vegas radiating the horizon. In no time we were there. But how do we end this ride? Vegas, in those days, was only a small promise of the real estate it would become, and so it wasn't long before I spotted a camper park right alongside the freeway, not too far from the downtown area.

"There!" I told the driver. "We're getting out over there at that campground."

He looked bewildered. "You wanna...get out here?" He pulled the car over and we scrambled out with our gear.

"Well, hey man, where you goin'? Dontcha think we should hang out s'more?"

My alarms started going off again. What the hell was he thinking?

"Nah, we haven't much money and this looks like the cheapest place in town to me," I prattled.

In no time we were sneaking into the campground, glad to be rid of this guy. I think that if he hadn't been so tired from the drive there might have been some sort of altercation—I'm not sure what. Did he have a gun? Did he want sex? We had rolled the "bones" for a moonlight drive to Las Vegas with a lonely skeleton. Luckily, we got sevens.

Stuck in Vegas

The campground was strictly for RV's; rows and rows of tinned vacationers on wheels. They had come to try their luck and feed the money machine with their hard-earned savings. We walked past the empty entry booth, ignored the after-hours instructions for payment, and located a small rectangular plot between two trailers. We chucked our tent and packs on the side and threw open our sleeping bags for a couple of hours sleep on the designated gravel bed. It wasn't long before the sun reestablished its domain.

With our bags rolled up, and tucked back onto our packs, we stumbled into the downtown area hunting for breakfast. The architecture was extravagant. There was Vegas Vic, the famous neon cowboy who gives you a wink and a welcoming grin as he empties your wallet. Casinos were lit up even in the daytime. Eventually we found food for pretty cheap. Hotel rooms were also cheap because the casinos wanted people to stay as long as possible, thereby draining their pockets a little bit more. There were no clocks anywhere so patrons would lose their sense of time. My impression of these limitless interior spaces, filled with a cacophony of slot machines, was that the amateurs manning the one-armed bandits were all casino factory workers. A negative paycheck was dearly earned. Here's where the working class go to vacation, trading their real factory and office jobs for this one. How imaginative. Drinks were cheap, the better to grease the machine. A guy stood in front of a giant wheel of fortune, throwing silver dollars at the thing and pulling down its giant lever. He was drunk and out of control, yelling "Whoa!" as he pressed the lever one more time. Who knows how long he had been there? This was early morning! A girl, just as drunk, was hanging on him. I'm sure she brought him lots of good luck. I felt like I was in the Hell scene of the Bosch triptych, "The Garden of Earthly Delights."

After a quick breakfast, we headed back to the Las Vegas Freeway, our next destination Salt Lake City. I was beyond exhaustion at this point and not having a hat was taking its toll. My head was badly burned. I was walking in a daze. I have no idea why I hadn't thought to buy a hat. I bought a bottle of Orange Crush instead and was amazed at how good it was. I could have drunk gallons of it. We hiked for a while to the north side of town and staked out a spot. "Been here twelve hours," read a previous hitchhiker's scrawl on the back of a road sign. We stood there for hours; nobody was in any mood to pick up a couple of hitchhikers. There was desperation in those faces behind the steering wheel, and I had the feeling that everyone who passed us by had just lost a lot of money. They would be in no mood for further adventures with a couple of strangers. The party was over.

Eventually I noticed a slow-moving freight train not too far from where we stood. We walked over to it and watched the rumbling wheels squeal around a bend. Open boxcars glided past. It would be so easy. Just run along the side, throw the backpacks in, and climb aboard. We stared at it for some time…but where was it going? What if its destination was not ours? What if it was only going to some obscure place in the desert for no apparent reason? If a boxcar door shuts, can you open it from the inside? (No.) What if we were stuck in the middle of this desert, inside a boxcar, that was hotter than an oven? Or what if some train yard "bull" out in the middle of nowhere decided to beat the shit out of you before handing you over to the authorities. Or what if we just got ticketed and had to give up more money? There were too many "what ifs." Plus, my crazy friend Billy broke his leg once jumping from a train. I couldn't do it. We walked back to the road sign.

It was midafternoon, still no rides, and I started to have symptoms of dehydration. All my joints ached and the veins in my body felt like they were fizzing or on fire. I was really out of it.

"I can't do this anymore. I've got to get out of this heat…this sun…" I said.

"Let's go back into town and get a hotel room," Jewell said.

I strode into the first hotel we saw, booked a room, and flopped on the bed in a nice dark air-conditioned space. It was early evening in heaven.

When I awoke, it was night—the next day! I had slept for over twenty-four hours. Jewell was beside herself.

"I didn't know if you were dead or what to think," she said. "I almost went for a doctor."

I felt quite refreshed.

"We won't be able to hitch out of here," I said. "How much money do we have left?"

"Less than three hundred dollars."

"Let's see how much plane tickets would be to Salt Lake."

In the morning we checked out of the hotel and headed for the nearby airport. But before getting there, Jewell stopped in front of a casino. "Wait here," she commanded. I had no idea what she was up to. Two minutes later she was back on the street with a very solemn look on her face.

"What's going on?"

"I just lost a dollar."

"You mean you went in there and squandered what little money we have?"

"I thought I'd get lucky for a change!"

I was angry but I stuffed it. After all, I'd been the victim of magical thinking all my life. The sirens of Las Vegas had clutched another victim.

"Nice try," I said.

We took a city bus to the airport terminal and purchased tickets; the total cost was a hundred dollars and well worth it.

Overwhelming relief washed over me as we settled into our seats. The view from the plane showed Las Vegas for what it truly is—an island of fantasy in a Martian landscape. It looked ridiculous. It shouldn't be there. And thank God we weren't either.

Flying over the desert was a joy. After a while I looked out the window and saw what I thought was a large crater. Was I seeing things? Are there craters in Nevada? Wasn't there a nuclear test site somewhere out here? But how could it be so close to Las Vegas? I decided I was seeing things. I closed my eyes and sunk back into the seat.

"Didn't you tell me you lived out here...somewhere?" Jewell asked.

"Uhm, yeah, Utah. My first three years of life were in Utah."

"Do you ever think about your father?"

"Elroy? I try not to."

"No, your real dad."

"Oh, yeah, my real dad. Sometimes."

"Do you think he's still out here, in that big desert down there?"

"Who knows? I haven't the slightest idea."

"Wouldn't you like to know?"

"Yeah, I guess I would. But that's like trying to find a needle in a haystack. And, anyway, at this point, what would it matter?"

"Just to know your own history," Jewell said. "Like, who is he? What's he like? Does he have a family?"

"Yeah, I guess. But I've heard a lot of stories about him anyway."

"From your crazy mother who you don't even get along with. If she had been a decent person, you wouldn't have lost contact with him. You'd know who he was, as a person. You could make up your own decisions about him."

"Yeah, I guess I don't understand her; or maybe I understand too much. She's so damn weird."

"She never understood you either; neither of them did."

"Well, Elroy especially. I was already a person when he appeared on the scene."

"You were a person when you were born. Children come as they are; they come *through* their parents, they're not little extensions of them."

"Well, I could never live near them again, that's for sure."

"Can't blame you," Jewell said. "Don't worry, we'll find someplace to settle."

The American Prairies

Salt Lake City, from the air, is a beautiful agate; an oasis where the aggregate of desert minerals meet their great dissolution through water. I took it as a sign that we would be safe, now that we were in the land of water. The alchemy of our voyage could be changed by this primordial element.

At the airport it was easy to catch Interstate 80, running just to the south end of it. I-80 runs east to west and divides the country roughly in half, with a little more emphasis into the north and straight through the Midwest. In fact, I-80 would take us through Rock Island where my grandparents and all my other relatives lived. Looking at our atlas, I noticed that the interstate system, east to west, is laid out numerically with the lowest, I-40, being in the south and I-90 in the north. Having seen *Easy Rider*, we were not so inclined to take I-40.

Riding out from the airport, I saw that the landscape was still semi-desert but there were clumps of tall grass spaced about a foot apart from each other. This meager offering of vegetation was all I needed to feel safe and hopeful. I was starting to feel more at home (wherever that was). We had several good rides from folks who were quite friendly and had a positive outlook on life. A couple of them were truckers; eighteen wheelers. It seems there were only two trucks worth having; you were either a Peterbilt owner or a Kenworth. These rides were pretty bumpy and loud with everyone shouting about themselves and where they were headed over the noise and the ubiquitous country-western station. You felt like you were on top of the world. I could see how truckers might feel like they own the place when they're in top gear and roaring down the highway.

Our last ride that day took us into the night. We had crossed over into Wyoming and were glad to be away from any desert. The driver, another hippie, asked if we needed a place to crash. He pulled up to his house a little way off the road and offered the use of his pickup for sleeping, so I took the truck bed and Jewell curled up on the "luxury" of the cab seat. I lay on my back and gazed up at the stars. They were so close you could reach out and touch them. In fact, before falling asleep, I reached out my hand and pretended to feel them; their gossamer nebulosity was so rich. The stars "spoke" to me again in the same way they had when I was a drunken three year old, "*Well, here you are.*" I fell asleep thinking of how a glance up to the sky was a glance into eternity. Or to look anywhere, really, was to look in the direction of an unfathomable void. Even looking at the bed of the truck, stuck as it was to the earth, was to look in the direction of a vast forever since the Earth was just something in the way of the view. We are, incredibly, marooned on a grain of sand. How is it we take ourselves so seriously?

The dawn's cadmium strokes found us fidgeting through our packs for some breakfast; I pulled out the trusty bag of granola.

"Hey, there's a diner not too far down the road," our host said walking towards the truck. "I can drop you there on my way to work."

"Sounds good!" As usual, we were starving.

After breakfast it was back on the road and a couple of good rides until we got stuck somewhere around Rawlins in the late afternoon. I saw, in the distance, a lonely figure walking our way. It was a fellow vagabond, strutting along with a crumpled canvas backpack. He was hitching in the opposite direction, on the other side of the road. He came over, sniffed at our state-of-the-art backpacks, with their aluminum frames and hip harnesses, and said, "You're not real hobos. If you were real hobos you'd have a pack like mine." Well, you can't please everyone. If we had ditched our fancy backpacks he would have scooped them up. To be frank, he looked a little too plump to be a hobo; he was disheveled enough, but with no real signs of wear and tear. He was just another lost soul like the rest of us and not, assuredly, a gentleman of the road. Neither was I (nor did I want to be). But like me, he was a searcher; searching for what we'll never know. I'm sure he didn't know himself, or that he was even aware of the fact that he was searching for something. Perhaps it was just for a patch for that hole in his psyche. We watched him disappear into the west.

Our next ride would take us to the other side of Laramie. Evening was starting to set in, and again, our driver asked if we needed a place to stay. We said sure, that would be great, and he turned off the highway. He was another long-hair and lived with a communal group of friends down a dusty red road. There were maybe four or five men and two women living in this small house that was tucked back into a lovely pine cove. The guy told us there was a place out back to set up our tent upon a small hill. That night we were invited to supper and offered a bowl of chili. The conversation was lively and amiable; people wanting to know where we were from and where we were going. Everyone was easy and natural. After dinner someone put on a record and passed a few joints around. I wasn't much of a Dave Mason fan until the "J" went by for the second time. My God—how could I have ignored Dave Mason?! I can still hear that opening guitar chime of "Shouldn't Have Took More Than You Gave," splintering the air while the searing wah-wah at the bridge sliced through my brain and blew me out of the room. Music, like sex or food, was a different animal on pot.

A crimson sun was setting, emblazing the walls through the open windows. I was pretty relaxed and just plain dog tired from the day. We helped with the dishes and then stumbled out to our tent through the darkled piney undergrowth and passed out.

In the morning we used our host's facilities, had breakfast with them, and headed back to I-80. We got a ride right away to Cheyenne and then had a nice long ride with an academic from Boston. He was a seismologist involved in research. A lively discussion ensued about what would normally have been a very boring landscape. I had to agree with how our Canadian friend, Derrick, felt about the plains; they were best traversed in an all-night run. The professor told us of how dynamic the land is and how it continuously fluctuates. That, if we could make a time-lapsed movie spanning the centuries, these rolling treeless hills would appear to be rippling up and down, up and down. The earth was alive. It was nice to talk to someone intelligent for a change, and there was little need to go into the usual song and dance routine. Jewell later thought he reminded her of the Mad Hatter in *Alice in Wonderland*. He did have a madness about him; a creative madness. When he dropped us off somewhere in Nebraska he hugged Jewell, kissed her on the neck, shook my hand and wished us well. The man turned down a nondescript asphalt road and quickly disappeared, like the White Rabbit down the hole. Jewell said she felt a sexual vibe from him. I didn't notice anything untoward. Maybe it was wishful thinking on her part from the neck peck. I think she related to him more than I did; she was attracted to men who could show a bit of erudition.

We were stranded now, God knows where, in the quiet green countryside somewhere in Nebraska. It was a good long ride from Cheyenne and I was sure we weren't too far from Iowa. We were still on I-80 but it was late in the day and there were hardly any cars; just a long cement ribbon stretching at once from the past and into the future. We decided to set up the tent at the bottom of an embankment next to the road and forget about it. There was nothing out there to hide us, but at this point in our excursions, we didn't care anymore. No one would see us in our orange tent because there was no one there! In the early dawn I had the strangest dream that I was being walked over by crowds of people. They were all murmuring and talking about something. I awoke confused and terrified because the dream was continuing, even as I lay there. I quickly became alarmed hearing all this commotion outside the tent. Was it the cops? Are we getting busted for trespassing? Unzipping the flap, I was confronted with the face of a cow! We were in the middle of a herd that had somehow crossed the barbed wire fence. There must have been a dozen black and white cows all munching breakfast around our tent. They were unperturbed, pulling up grass with their soft purse-like muzzles; gently moving away as we broke camp. A quick bite to eat and we were ready for our next ride. We always carried bread, peanut butter, fruit, granola, sometimes cheese, and a boiled egg or two.

Another hippie van picked us up and took us through Lincoln, dropping us off a little way into Iowa. And then we caught another ride in another van with two other hitchhikers, floundering as usual, in the seat-less cargo area. This ride was headed for Illinois. Not much was said—these Midwesterners were a tight-lipped bunch. But when we dropped the two off in Des Moines the driver introduced himself and said that he was headed for Chicago. Normally that would have been a great ride but I wanted to stop in Rock Island and see my grandparents, Genny and Del. Our driver had a CB radio and called around to see if he could hook us up with a trucker going east from there.

"Breaker, breaker one-niner Hey y'all, I got a couple of thumbers in need of a ride, anyone headed for the Big Apple?"

Shhhhhk...pop..."Ten-nine...was...thak?"... kshhhhhhk

"Need a driver for two thumbers goin' east in a coupla days anyone?"

Kshhhhhhhk...pop...shk."Copy that...I'm goin' west to Idiot Island but my brother in Moline's goin' east, four-ten?"

"Affirmative, threes and eights, catch you on the flip side."

He made a connection for us with a guy whose brother makes runs from Moline to New York on a regular basis. His handle was "Sugarman." Sugarman hauled strawberries. We were delighted. The trucker gave us his brother's phone number and said he would be leaving in three days. Just enough time to see Grandma and be on our way. As we got closer to the Quad Cities, I started having second thoughts about seeing my relatives. I don't think Jewell was up for it either. We would, after all, be presenting ourselves at a disadvantage. Jewell and I had come down to visit a couple of years ago, when we were students, looking so full of promise as young people often do when they appear to be thoughtfully engaged in their future—now we were just bums, lost souls, hippies. I could hear them asking how come we weren't married and paying a mortgage and buying a new car—all purchased, of course, from my job as an accountant with kids on the way while my wife bakes cookies at home barefoot and in the kitchen…

Jewell started to cry a little.

"What's the matter?" I whispered.

"It's nothing."

"Doesn't look like nothing…"

"I'm just happy to be here…to see the Midwest again."

"Yeah, it looks pretty familiar, for sure."

"It looks like Minnesota here," she said.

I had never known her to cry from being happy; she wasn't a "happy" crier. Despite her claims of preferring urban life when she was a student, Jewell was a small-town girl at heart. She had a lot of friends in Minnesota, people that she had grown up with. I had friends too but not as many. The way my family moved around always made me the "new kid." I was a bit of a loner. Perhaps I should have paid more attention to her need for community. I don't know how we ever evolved to our present situation; how the dynamics of our relationship had catapulted us into where we were now. Maybe we had always misread each other. She never should have come with me to California and I never should have agreed to this flight east. But here we were at seven a.m. at the crossroads, I-80 and Dylan's infamous Highway 61. I called Grandma from a phone booth and she came to pick us up. She was surprised and thought we were still in Richmond. I hadn't written to tell her we were going on the road again.

The Quad Cities

It was early afternoon when we arrived in Davenport, Iowa, just a little south of I-80 on Highway 61. Grandma picked us up near the Oasis Drive-in Theater, a wonderful old drive-in we went to in the early 60s; I couldn't believe it was still there. We drove across the Government Bridge, past the arsenal, into Rock Island where my grandparents lived. Although the house looked the same, and even smelled the same from Grandma's cooking, it wasn't the same. The air of festivity that surrounded our family holidays had dissipated. Now it was just a dark theater, off season, waiting for the curtain to go up. We stored our backpacks upstairs in the spare bedroom and then Jewell went outside, leaving me with my grandmother. Visiting my grandparents was not as easy as I had hoped. When I was growing up, Grandma always supported me. Now it seemed as if she was siding with my parents. We went into the living room, with its pastel green walls, and sat on the gray sofa. Old glass in the windows gave a warped view of the outside world.

"You really hurt your mother when you left for California," she said.

"Yeah, I'm sure," I said.

"She was absolutely hysterical."

"I can imagine."

"Your father doesn't know what to do with her either."

I could offer a few suggestions, I thought to myself.

"And why are you doing this? Don't you know hitchhiking is dangerous?"

"I'm aware of the risks, Grandma."

"When I was your age, I wasn't afraid of a little hard work."

"I'm not either," I lied.

"I don't know what you think you're going to accomplish with all this gallivanting around. I've worked hard all my life to get where I am. That's what you do."

And where did it get you? I thought to myself again. Work hard for whom? Yourself? Or Mr. Boss Man who tried to screw Grandpa out of a pension when the factory was going under? Hitler was a hard worker too. Hard work, in and of itself, is not a virtue; it's just hard. Hard work without intention or a decent reward is fruitless. Hard work with no imagination is pitiful. Art is hard work. And even then you can work hard in your studio and no one will give a damn. Don't tell me about hard work in this country with its "American Dream." It's all a ruse. I wished I'd been born in Europe; some place with culture. I was silent. I didn't know what to say to her. There was a distancing I'd never felt before. It felt awkward, as if my grandmother didn't know who I was.

"We have a ride out of here if that makes you feel any better," I said.

"Well, that's good. When?"

"In three days. We're supposed to call a trucker over in Moline to set it up."

She softened. "I'm happy to hear it. Let's have fun while you're here. I know your aunts and uncles would love to see you again. What would you like for supper?"

"Anything, you're the greatest cook in the world."

She patted my face and left the room. I went out to Jewell who was sitting on the front steps.

"So how'd it go?" she asked.

"Great…just fine…happy to be here."

"I heard part of it."

"Oh, yeah, well…whatever," I said. "We'll be out of here in three days anyway."

"Can't wait," she said.

Staying at my grandparent's house stirred up all sorts of nostalgia. I couldn't believe she still had my childhood toothbrush, in its original tube with the blue elephant cap, tucked away in the medicine cabinet. Even the damp smell of earth beneath the oak trees in their backyard brought forth innumerable childhood memories. I was haunted. Here were the Thanksgivings and Christmas feasts with the grandkids at the overflow card table where we sat, even into our late teens, jiggling the table with our knees for a laugh. There were Sunday dinners, with men congregating in the kitchen, smoking cigarettes and building a metropolis of empty beer bottles on the table while the women drifted to the living room with their highballs and the latest Hollywood gossip. We kids would watch Disney's Wonderful World of Color on a black-and-white set or else go ice-skating across the street in the lamplight while doo-wop played on loudspeakers and folks warmed themselves at a fire that roared out of a rusted oil drum. I loved to hear Grandma recite Tennyson's "The Charge of the Light Brigade." She had committed it to memory from her childhood. I'd ask her on occasion to recite it, and she would immediately start hamming it up, going into a wild and comic flare that would have us all rolling on the floor with laughter. Such was the family theater in blue-collar Rock Island, Illinois in the early 1960s.

Not being married, Jewell and I had to sleep in separate beds. I don't know what my grandmother thought was going to happen but it's her house so "them's the rules."

On the next evening, we were taken out to dinner. I was having a good time but noticed that Jewell was becoming a bit sullen. I couldn't figure it out. We went for a walk before bedtime. The atmosphere was warm and thick, a slight breeze wafting the lush river valley air. We got into an argument.

"We have to get the hell out of here," she said.

"Yeah, I know, tomorrow we'll set it up with 'Sugarman.'"

"Even if we can't set it up, we have to get out regardless."

"Why?"

"Because Grandma and Grandpa can't afford to be putting us up; we're eating them out of house and home."

"Oh bullshit, we just got here."

"Look, they took us out to dinner. We're costing them. And Grandma's overwhelmed having to cook for four people," she said.

"We can't just leave. Grandma's planning on having some relatives over before we go.

"And won't that be fun," she said. "We'll be the talk of the town, and aren't you just having the time of your life."

Jewell was embarrassed to be seen in such a bad light as this. But I was determined to stick it out until the ride came through. I didn't want my grandmother to have to drop us back on I-80 after assuaging her fears with a dependable ride.

"You know, I am really sick and tired of you running the show. The only reason we're even on the road again is because of you!" I said.

"That's not what you said in California. You agreed with me and said you wanted to leave too."

"I said it to make you happy…what else was I supposed to do?" I asked.

"Well, aren't you the martyr!" she said.

"Shut up! These are my people and I'll handle it my way. We'll leave when I damn well please!"

Jewell fumed; her silence deafening.

When we got back to the house, I opened the *I Ching* and threw the coins. I was no longer using it as a "cosmic compass" but rather as a tool for deciphering my relationship with Jewell; someone I was starting to see in a different light. Again, the hexagram of Chung Fu / Inner Truth popped up. There was a lot of incomprehensible jabber in this hexagram that didn't seem to apply to the situation at hand, but then there was a *movement* at the third line that caught my eye. It said that when a man's strength lies outside of himself, and particularly in relation to someone else, he is tossed between joy and sorrow no matter how close one may be to the other person. The *I Ching* was pointing out my codependency with Jewell. I was sorry to have yelled at her but I was also tired of taking orders. What was happening to us? We'd had our fights before but this was different. I wasn't so sure we'd survive as a couple after this trip.

The next day I called up "Sugarman" only to be told I had the wrong number. Either we got the phone number wrong from the radio static or his brother mixed it up. This was bad for a couple of reasons, one being the obvious, but also it would have been much more reassuring for my grandmother if we had what could reasonably be construed as a safe passage. We would definitely have to be moving along now.

On the fourth day, after breakfast, Grandma gave me a peculiar, almost sorrowful look, and said, "I want to show you something." Jewell and I followed her to the living room. She pointed us to the sofa, headed upstairs and said, "I'll be right back." She brought down a small box, opened it, took out a clump of yellowing photos and spread them out on the coffee table. "I don't know if I should show you these... don't tell your mother." Grandma had a bunch of those old pictures of George; some I had seen before from my mother's collection and some I had never seen.

"Oh wow. You know, Grandma, I've seen some of these."

"You have?"

"Yeah, Mom showed 'em to me a few years ago."

"Well, that's a surprise."

"Look at this one," Jewell said. It was a picture of me on a rocking horse, holding a Tootsie Pop, lips rouged from the cherry candy; mittens dangling from my sleeve on a string that my mother always fastened to my coat. Jewell was being tender again; arguments forgotten.

"Yeah, so, what was George like, Grandma?" I asked.

"He treated your mother very badly. He was always running around and getting drunk, chasing after other women. Thought himself a bigshot."

"Gee, but he doesn't look like that in these pictures. I mean, here he is holding me up in the air with a big smile and all…"

"He wanted to get rid of your mother so he could marry the boss's daughter!"

That seemed oddly funny to me, I don't know why. It sounded like a cartoon—not real.

"Now when you two get settled somewhere I'll send these to you. It's not right that you don't have some kind of family history…even if he was a scallywag! But don't tell your mother and don't you go doing what she did."

"What did she do?" I spoofed.

"She looked up her biological father, my old ex, and she was very upset that she did." My grandmother had divorced a man I never met who was an alcoholic and beat her. But this was news concerning my mother. After years of disparaging remarks about my actual father, and thwarting any discussion about him, here she was satisfying her curiosity about her own father. This hypocrisy was too much.

"Why was she upset?"

"She said that when she introduced herself to him, he took her by the hand and said, 'Now that you've found me, don't ever go away.' Needless to say, she never went back."

"That's it?"

"Well, it spooked her."

Yeah, my mother is spooky alright, I thought to myself. "So...did it bother you that she looked him up, Grandma?" I asked.

"No, why should it? Anyway, she didn't tell me about it until years later."

"Well, I don't think it would be very easy to find George anyway," I said.

Grandma lent us her car that day and we drove around my old haunts across the river in Davenport. The small gray house where I spent my childhood was still there with its two glorious silver maples dwarfing it. Funny how a tree can make a house—if you took them away, the house would be a shack.

"So, this is where you lived after your mother's divorce?" Jewell asked.

"Yup. Man, lots of memories here…"

Standing in front of the old house again I remembered when my mother and I first moved in and how we had no refrigerator for a while; spoiled milk, tasting like vomit, sat on the shelf for a couple of days. And we had no car because one day she refused to drive anymore for fear of causing an accident and not wanting the responsibility of having to choose between a life or death scenario involving fantasized situations. She never drove again for the rest of her life and would consider this one of her virtues. We took the bus. Eventually she got a job as a secretary and found that the old woman living next door was taking on new clients for what would now be called daycare but back then was simply a more comprehensive form of babysitting. I pointed to her house, covered in the same gray slate as mine, and told Jewell about her.

"We called her 'Grandma-Next-Door,'" I said.

"What was her real name?"

"Daisy Erpst, or Erps, something like that. She was quite a character."

Daisy was built like a Sherman tank camouflaged in a dress. The woman propelled herself in deep-sea-diver shoes that were open-toed; a mustard gas of bromodosis emanating from her feet. She was strict but had a soft side as well. She fed me second breakfasts and lunch, much to my mother's alarm since she did not want to pay more for food (I wondered now what I would have done for lunch?). Daisy assured my mother the cost would not be extra. She was an extraordinary cook;

chicken and dumplings were her specialty. She also made fried calves' brains, the first and last I'd ever tasted. Her kitchen was the hub of the house, the aroma of frying food was non-stop. Every week a dark-blue farm truck would stop in the alley where groceries could be purchased. It carried all sorts of produce from a family farm somewhere out in the country. I would hop onto the rear fender of this 1930s or 40s pickup and stick my nose into the fragrant strawberries, glistening in the sun.

The kids on our block were river town scrappers—the spawn of working-class toughs. If I was at home and playing outside with my toys, they would descend like a flock of starlings, grab stuff, and inevitably break something. When I was under Daisy's care, she wouldn't allow me to play with the neighborhood kids for fear of me getting hurt. She was afraid that if I broke an arm, she would not get paid. Consequently, I had to amuse myself by drawing all day. She couldn't keep me supplied in enough paper so I was given only one, rarely two, sheets with which to engage a child's penchant for play—via abstraction and imagination. I dreamed whole episodes of imaginary adventures crammed into two sides of a single sheet of paper. On days when there was no new paper a palimpsest was forged.

"So you didn't have anyone to play with? Sounds awful."

"Well, I wasn't completely devoid of a social life. All sorts of her relatives, young and old, sauntered through. One kid I remember in particular. He was a few years older than me, not much more than eight or nine. I was afraid of him."

"Why?"

"One day he drew an angel and tore a hole in its chest exclaiming, 'Look! I tore its heart out!' That freaked me out. That guy had problems. Now that I think about it, it was rather creative in an *enfant terrible* sort of way."

"So, was there a Grandpa-Next-Door?"

"Oh, yeah, Carl. That was her husband; he was a junkman…worked at the city dump."

Carl brought home all kinds of tchotchkes that the tide of trash washed up at his feet: rings of skeleton keys, dime store figurines, a conch shell doorstop, doorknobs, and a white marble egg that magically altered your senses by its unexpected weight. There were so many figurines clamoring for attention in such little space that dusting had to be relegated via territorial per diems. Mondays belonged to the living room, Tuesdays to the kitchen, Wednesdays for the back sewing room, etc. I loved all this clutter and decided I would be a junkman when I grew up. The richness of incongruous flotsam everywhere created a magical world that would nurture my imagination. Going from junkman to artist is just a side-step away. Carl would come home on hot days and take his shirt off, exposing an undershirt that was brown stained from the rotten garlic bag that hung around his neck. I assumed he wore it for the purpose of health or to keep the devil away. Daisy would pour his coffee into a faux jadeite cup and a saucer into which he would pour the hot creamy liquid, cooling it for consumption; coffee was slurped from the saucer.

When I started going to school, he would bring me along to help with one of his gigs—picking up trash with a pick and bag at a local restaurant in the mornings. I was seven years old and it was my first job. I picked up garbage for half an hour every day before walking eight blocks to school. On cold mornings the restaurant staff would pay me in hot chocolate. They thought I was cute. Carl would also pay me, every once in a while, in cheap toys and trinkets from a dime store or things he would make in his shop out of wood and paint. I appreciated the handmade stuff the best. He did play a mean trick on me though by nailing a dime into his porch and telling me I could have it if I could pick it up. After trying a few times, I figured it out but I still continued to pluck at it—half out of a sense of play and willingness to appease an adult, and half out of magical thinking, that the dime, against all odds, might actually slide out, Excalibur style. My fingernails were chipped and shredded, much to my mother's dismay, which prompted a tongue lashing at Carl. But one day when I was playing in my yard a fluff of dandelion seed came floating by, glowing silver in the afternoon sun, and something told me to follow it. I was curious to see where it might land. It floated around on a lazy current of air, almost making a complete circle of the house, before slowly descending onto the lawn where it landed right on top of a dime! So I got my dime after all—a lesson in trusting the universe.

One good thing about Carl though is that he could play a mean polka. Whenever the spirit hit him, he would pull out his accordion and play while sitting on the bottom stairs inside his house. The stairs leading to the second floor were enclosed like a hallway, and that enclosure could amplify sound. So when he played, he would open the windows at the top and flood the neighborhood with music. I asked him once what song he was playing and he said he was making it up as he went along. I'm not sure if that was true but I can still hear him, dancing the sun down, on a sultry summer's day in this little river town long, long ago...

Jewell looked at me strangely, "Hey, Mr. Nostalgia..." She was teasing me but her tone was such that I wasn't sure if it really bothered her or not; I knew I was being indulgent but, I didn't know if I'd ever be back here. I began to realize that light was different in the various places one lived and that, like the light in California, this light was a memory trap as well; memories waiting for their release.

"Don't you ever get nostalgic?" I asked.

"No. Well, maybe. But not like you."

"What?"

"You get so consumed; and sometimes you get really sad. How can you possibly remember things from when you were five? I think you remember things wrong...or else make it up as you go along."

"It happened. What can I say?"

"You should be thinking about *now*, about our situation and our future, instead of wallowing around in the past."

"I'm not wallowing. I haven't thought about this place in years."

169

"You are *always* like this. And why would you even want to look at your old house again? I thought those were painful times for you."

"Yeah...but some good times too."

We drove to my old grade school, Johnson Elementary. I walked around the front of it and had to stop every once in a while to let it all sink in. Like a gift, the doors were open so we perused the floors; large empty rooms with large doors and towering windows. The smell of chalk dust and the highly polished wooden halls still creaked with each step. Images from the past lived here: crayons and manila paper; *Basic Readers* showing rosy cheeked cherubs with buttery hair. A tour through the basement led to the gym where an odor that will never be eradicated lingered. It was a mixture of coal dust and sour milk from the small milk cartons that were sold and the old coal-burning furnace, now long gone, that had kept us warm in winter. The gym doubled as a lunchroom when the long metal tables were unfolded out from the wall. Our janitor, a Mr. Sueur, would sit on the stage and peel apples for any kid who didn't like apple skins. It became a thing. I think the kids just liked having some attention.

"We should probably be getting back," Jewell said.

"Yeah...prepare yourself."

That evening we were visited by relatives. They had all come for the sideshow. As was expected, everyone was awkward. It had only been a couple of years since I had seen them but so much had happened to me that it seemed like centuries. There was a real generation gap back then; a drawing of the lines. People from my generation were, in general, in a state of social/cultural revolt against almost everything our parents stood for. The system was a failure. But we didn't really have anything to take its place either. We were just who we are. Trust us. My cousins on the other hand, who were my age, were not in revolt; they were just replicas. Their reach for the ring on the merry-go-round of life was short. Strange smiles from strange people. I don't think they understood that we weren't out on some frivolous lark. We were just trying to find a home, someplace where we could fit in—or at least I was. I envied them. They had no need to break free and had strong family ties. They didn't grow up with a step-parent that you had to stumble over and around, avoiding them as if in a drunken dance. And they also couldn't understand how serious we were about art and literature. In Plato's *The Republic*, he bids civilians to praise the artist who comes to their town but don't let him stay. Crown him with a wreath and send him on his way, for he is a bad influence. I guess we were too much stimulation for these sleepy people. For me, the Midwest was no longer home and my community was waiting elsewhere. Jewell was just glad to be away from the West Coast.

Uncle Arnie, after hearing our hitchhiking stories, gave us five dollars and said, "You should write a book!"

Yeah, I thought, that's not gonna happen... Aunt Mary started weeping as they went out the door. Good grief, I'm not dead, just not what you'd like to see.

That night I had a chance to talk to my grandfather about his life. Del was born in Moline, and he was a cop's kid. He used to go around with his father on patrol and meet all sorts of petty criminals and roustabouts down by the river.

Del taught me to play pool. He had a funny way of holding the cue stick, resting it in the crux of his forefinger and double-jointed thumb.

"My dad owned a pool hall," he said. "I was shootin' pool when I was seven years old."

"Yeah, you were good, Grandpa. I remember that time you took me over to your friend's house, with that antique pool table he had; the one with the woven leather pockets and the Greek columns for legs."

"Yeah, that was an antique alright; don't know how he ever got it in the house."

"So you must have met quite a few characters in pool halls back in the day?" I asked.

"Oh yeah," he said. "I was friends with a guy who was the boot runner for a mobster named Looney."

"Boot runner?"

"Bootlegger. You know, prohibition. A boot runner goes out and picks up the hootch. Gangs from Chicago would drop off the stuff and this guy I knew would drive out of town to pick it up and lug it home to Looney. I used to go with him, just for the ride."

"Wow. But you were a cop's kid!"

"Yeah," he smiled.

"So, how'd he get a nickname like 'Loony'...how crazy was he?"

"Looney was his name! John Patrick Looney. He was just a gangster that lived in Rock Island. He owned a newspaper, the *Rock Island News*—not the *Argus*—and he used to publish his competitors' family histories and double dealings. Some other folks too, people he didn't like. He'd blackmail 'em. Chicago mobsters were afraid of him."

"Wow."

"Yeah, there was a lot of bad stuff going on back then. I went to pick up Mildred one night after work, that's my first wife, and we ended up in the middle of a shootout."

"That is crazy."

"Rock Island had a lot of gang wars going on back then; you'd be surprised."

"So Mildred was your first wife?"

"Yeah. She passed away; died of a stroke at forty-seven."

"I'm sorry, that must have been rough."

"Yeah, but then I never woulda met Genny. Or you!"

Our conversation drifted. He told me to finish school and I told him, "Maybe, you never know."

"Don't end up like me," he said. "I never even finished high school."

"Why didn't you finish high school, Grandpa?"

"Aw, I was expelled."

"For what?"

But he refused to tell me; he was too embarrassed to talk about it all these years later. And he took that secret to his grave.

I loved Del, even though he was buddies with Elroy. I suppose he was a surrogate father for Elroy, who hated his alcoholic father. Maybe he was like an older brother he could look up to; a replacement for the one who ran away. Del would always vouch for him and say he was a "good man." Grandpa was the salt of the earth and treated my grandmother well.

We left the next day. Grandma drove us back to our port of entry on I-80. I pulled out my sign for N.Y. and we waved our goodbyes. I was both sad and happy to get out of there. She gave us fifty dollars, God bless her.

Hexagram 56: Lü / The Wanderer

We had a few false starts out of Davenport; meandered below and around Chicago; got left high and dry on I-80 from which we earned a warning from a nice cop; and then—bingo! We caught a ride all the way to upstate New York via I-90 with "Reefer Man" Mike and his truck escort service. "Reefer Man" didn't have any reefer…and we could have used it seeing how his car was constantly swerving from a broken shock pin— tossing gas out of a punctured tank every time we hit a bump. The car reeked of gasoline, B.O., and cheese puffs. The steering wheel creased his belly. He made a living driving back and forth on whatever interstate he happened to be on after a run, calling out on his CB to any trucker in the area in need of an escort. There was a continuous supply of snacks laid out across the dashboard: cheese and peanut butter cracker packages, potato chips, Twinkies; lots of empty cellophane blowing about the cabin from an open window.

"Care for a pork rind?" he said, proffering the bag under my nose.

"Uhm, no thanks."

We talked about his business and had a few laughs; a decent fellow really. Escorts are used for wide loads—the escort service gets a certain amount per mile. He didn't seem to be getting any takers. I couldn't imagine being ensconced behind a wheel, calling out on a CB for possible work, in an endless, and possibly fruitless, drive. I didn't think his handle, "Reefer Man," was doing him any favors either. Who wants a stoned escort service for a wide load? It was also fairly obvious he wasn't exactly a registered escort, nor was his vehicle up to code.

Mike was headed home, and I was very glad to be going straight through these metropolitan areas that sprawled around Toledo and Cleveland. Hitching through there would have been problematic and I didn't want any more trouble with cops. After a long drive, he finally dropped us off in some obscure place outside of Ripley, New York. From there we got a few local rides to Westfield, home of the original Welch's Grape Juice Company. We learned this from a librarian when we walked into the Patterson Library, asking for directions. I'm not sure how the subject came up. We slid out of our packs, propped them against her desk, and gazed at this surprisingly beautiful building—ionic columns outside at the entrance, golden Corinthian capped columns forming a circle inside. I wanted to get away from the lake and go deeper into New York so we started thumbing NY State Route 394 south towards I-86. It was getting late in the day and we needed to find a place to crash.

Our next ride would take us to Jamestown. The driver was young, probably our age, and part owner of a local vineyard. He was very enthusiastic about his business, explaining the intricacies of grape growing and being a vintner. New York wines were a burgeoning business in 1976 and he was excited to be getting in on the ground floor, learning his craft.

He offered us a spare bedroom in his apartment. After traveling from sunup to sundown, we were quite grateful and took him up on the offer. His apartment was a second-floor walkup above a nameless storefront. It was one of those buildings you see squeezed into a triangle from an irregular shaped intersection—a miniature Flatiron Building of New York City fame. From the front it looked like a brick ship. His living room was in the prow where we listened to his vast collection of indigenous music. African drumming was on the menu along with spaghetti and glasses of red wine. He said he had to get up early the next day and showed us how to lock up when we left. Later, while retiring in our room, I went to use the bathroom and saw him preening in the mirror...stark naked. I didn't know what to think. He didn't like doors? Some people are just open with their bodies, and I'm no prude, but I do have boundaries. I suspected this to be a strange invitation of some sort. I told Jewell if she wanted to use the bathroom to approach with caution. We snickered about it and snuck around him. It rained that night; a soft shushing against the window. I saw lightning and was grateful to have a bed. I was also grateful to see lightning—something I hadn't seen in a long, long time. Traveling east was a reintroduction to water. After the dehydration of the desert, I never took water for granted again. I told myself I would collect plants when I finally threw down the anchor. Plants: those green living crystals that remember themselves into existence every summer.

The next morning, we had breakfast and cleaned up the kitchen for our host who had embarked into his day. Dishes glued with tomato sauce, as well as a weeklong clutter, were piled up in the sink; it was a bachelor's pad. We organized our gear and let ourselves out.

I liked the look of Jamestown, but I couldn't see how you would make a living there. Lots of old and abandoned brick buildings with brick streets. It was actually quite depressing and yet still retained a certain charm. Perhaps it reminded me of Rock Island. We got on I-86 and headed east. There were hardly any rides, and it took us all day to get to the Elmira-Horseheads area. I couldn't tell what was going on with the people we met. The strife and hardness were quite palpable, even from the folks who gave us rides. Was it the influence of New York City? It seemed the further east we went, the worse it got; there was a certain brutality in the air. The idea of living in NYC was not very appealing. Perhaps we could live an hour by train outside of it? Maybe an hour is too close. A chatty young woman gave us a short ride and said, "Have you been to Ithaca? It's really beautiful...lots of waterfalls and stuff.

Cornell University is there." We thought we would try it. But that night we were stranded in Elmira because we couldn't even get a thirty mile ride to Ithaca. We stayed at a Holiday Inn. There were no cheaper hotels.

I threw an *I Ching*. Where the hell should we go? Should we think about rural New York or head closer to the city? Head north or south? What should we be looking for? The response was: *Lü / The Wanderer*. No kidding, how crazy is that? Lots of good advice here: the wanderer's home is the road; no fixed abode, etc. Also, don't give yourself airs, be cautious and reserved, and be obliging towards others. The changing line, the one you need to really pay attention to, was a six in the fifth place. It spoke of finding a home in foreign lands and the importance of introducing oneself in the right way in order to find a "circle of friends." I went to bed that night astounded at the *I Ching* for addressing our given situation so accurately. But I wasn't sure about the specificity of that changing line — until the next day.

We were up bright and early, had our due continental breakfast, and staggered back to our post on NY State 13 to Ithaca. We got a ride right away with Nancy; the first friendly person we'd met since leaving Jamestown. We all had a lively conversation as we rambled through the lush green hills. She was freshly divorced and a blossoming feminist. It seemed as if we had known her all our lives.

As we came into Ithaca, we were welcomed by a huge John Birch Society billboard saying "America, Love It or Leave It."

"Whoa, check that out," I said.

"Yeah, unfortunately there are some real conservative pricks out here. It's a beautiful place to live though," Nancy said. We rode through town and out into the rolling countryside to her sister's home. They let us pitch our tent there for the night. We were invited to supper: homegrown asparagus, pork, rice with mushrooms and onions, and strawberry-rhubarb tarts for dessert. I don't remember her sister's name—I didn't write it down—but Sally was her older daughter and Tim her younger son. Sally was an art major and so a conversation was easily kindled. Tim was adventurous and listened wide-eyed to our hitchhiking stories. He had built a dome in the backyard and was working on a teepee so he "could be more mobile." The house was filled with antiques. Sally's great-great-grandfather was a traveling limner; examples of his work lay about the house. He would prepare slats of wood and then work the portraits of his customers onto the pre-painted bodies and backgrounds.

That night in the tent I offered my observations. "I think this is a good omen."

"What? You want to live here?" Jewell asked.

"Don't you think the hexagram I threw last night points to Ithaca? I mean, look, here we have nice people who took us in, fed us; like a *circle of friends.* I really connect with these folks."

"Yeah, it's a thought. But I think we should keep going. We can always come back if we don't see anything better," she said.

"Yeah, you're right, let's go see the Atlantic. We should be able to say we've seen the Pacific and the Atlantic. And then maybe we come back."

I slept rather fitfully that night. Was Ithaca the answer? In the morning, Nancy took us out for breakfast. She had some business to attend to concerning her divorce up in Cazenovia, about an hour away, and so we set off with her to see the rest of this green country. We drove past Cortland's endless orchards, up and over through Pompey, twisting around many corners, until we finally reached Cazenovia, situated at the end of a pretty little lake with its namesake. Cazenovia, like a lot of things in the east, was quite old, having been incorporated in 1810. It was the site of the Fugitive Slave Act Convention of 1850, organized in protest to the proposed Fugitive Slave Act that required escaped slaves to be returned to their masters in the South. Frederick Douglas was at the convention. In fact, many abolitionists were either born or lived there. It was a tiny town with a city park, so Nancy dropped us off there while she went about her business. We were tired as usual and found a grassy spot, propped ourselves against a concrete stormwater box, and took a snooze—just two hobos in the park. A couple of hours later she was back, picked us up and drove west across the state past the Finger Lakes, to the other end of Cayuga Lake. The weather was beginning to darken and we discussed places to stay. We wanted to keep out of the rain.

"There's a pretty park where my sister and I used to camp. They may have cabins for cheap; cheaper than a hotel anyway. Would you like to see it?" After meandering around the lake we came to Cayuga Lake State Park where we found ourselves in a primitive cabin, waving goodbye to Nancy.

We were there for two days of rain, damp, and cold. We hadn't thought to replenish our food supply when we were driving around and had run out of food again. I saw a lot of full garbage cans after an extended weekend of revelry by the locals and decided to do a little dumpster diving. I felt like a cartoon cat, rummaging through garbage cans, using the lid for a tray of found fish bones. No, I didn't use the lid for a tray but I did find some perfectly usable items: a half carton of eggs, butter, and even a bit of wine. These sustained us long enough to gather up our things, put on some raingear, get the hell out of there and find a hotel in nearby Seneca Falls.

I don't know if it was the lack of food, or if it's just the state of strangeness one enters into when wandering free like this, but after a while the dual states of consciousness, dream and reality,   tend to mingle and lose their boundaries. Jewell said something to me, and I responded, but in between the something said and my response I spaced out and had this flash of an image that looked like a rectangle fitting mechanically into a lock. I have no idea what it meant. One could speculate that my unconscious self was communicating symbolically with my consciousness, telling me that I had to figure some things out concerning our current state of affairs...that this lock needed picking. Or maybe it was an image of a verbal exchange I was about to have with Jewell, brought on by hunger and sheer exhaustion, which seemed more likely.

We found a hotel in Seneca Falls and stayed for two more days of rain. After spending a year in a glorious California drought, and a harrowing trek through the desert, we were now drowning in this deluge that didn't seem to have an end. I looked out of our hotel window at the ceaseless gray sheets of rain, wondering how long it and our money would last, and if we could even think about hitching to the Atlantic on what little we had left.

"I'm tired of hitching," I said. "We need to get a car."

Jewell walked over to the window. The gray light, projected through the rain on the glass, streamed down her face.

"I agree. I'm sick of it myself."

"Can we ask your folks for some money to buy a car?"

"I've already asked Mom too many times. I can't keep asking her for money. And anyway, she has to sneak it to us because Dad doesn't approve of our 'living in sin.' It puts pressure on her."

"We could pay them back once we're settled," I said, "Christ, they make so much damn money."

Jewell thought for a moment and said, "Why don't I tell them we're getting married."

"Seriously? If you tell them that, then we'll have to get married."

"Yeah, so what? We'd be together anyway, it wouldn't matter. People do it all the time. It's nothing new."

I was a bit surprised at this since Jewell and I spelled marriage with a little "m." Being a feminist, she had always maintained that marriage was enslavement for women in a society run by men; the thought of being "owned" did not appeal to her. And I didn't give a damn about marriage either. We didn't need to have a piece of paper that told the world we were together. Consequently, we had never talked much about it. But it was true, if a marriage certificate offered advantages why not use one? And her confidence in saying that, "we'd be together anyway," was awfully sweet. It made me feel that we really were a unit, that we had a future, and that we could weather any situation—even if it included marriage.

"So…we're getting married so we can buy a car?" I asked.

"Yeah."

We were quiet for a moment. A long moment, and just kind of stared at each other waiting for the other to speak.

"What the hell, that's a great idea! Go ahead; lay it on 'em," I finally said.

She went to the lobby and called her mother to tell her the good news and, oh, by the way, could she please Western Union some money to us so we can buy a car and settle down? Her parents were ecstatic. They were going to foot the bill for a big wedding, they were going to fly right out there, they were going to make all sorts of big plans. And every other word from them was about coming "home" to Minnesota. They were out of their minds.

The next morning the rain had stopped. The piercing light of a new day made the wet trees glisten as if you could almost hear their leaves, tinkling like prisms in the wind. It had to be a good omen. Sure enough, Jewell's parents had sent the money to the hotel. I started thumbing through the want ads in the back of the local paper for a used car. For sale: 1960 Valiant, 60K miles, mechanically sound, needs some body work. We paid two hundred and ten dollars for that rust bucket with a bent front fender and that was too much. But I always liked the style of this little red car, and the push button transmission was a hoot. I was a little suspicious of it, seeing how strangely the owner smiled at us. I'm sure he was glad to have palmed it off on a stranger, someone he'd never see again. I didn't care, we had some money left over for insurance, gas and possibly parts—as long as it got us to the coast and back, that's all I cared about. Our hitchhiking days were over.

The next day, after picking up supplies, we left Seneca Falls in the afternoon and caught I-90 for our trip east. How nice to have a trunk—what a luxury! The car was heavy as a tank with a little straight six-cylinder engine that could hardly drag its sorry ass up a hill, but the engine was sound and steady as a tractor. We drove through Syracuse, Oneida, Utica, and then somewhere around Herkimer or Little Falls we split from 90 because the road started to bend south. We went straight across towards Saratoga Springs, home of the famous bottled mineral water and Skidmore College, and stayed that night in the great Adirondack Forest. We had driven out of the rain and found a peaceful campground there. The evening brought forth what I thought were mosquitos. They wouldn't bother you if you were near the fire but, wow, walk away from the fire and you were eaten alive. When we got into our tent we were still getting eaten alive. I pointed the flashlight at the mosquito netting and saw a tiny cloud of "something" pouring into the tent.

"Look at this!" I exclaimed.

"What the hell is that?"

"I have no idea—head for the car!"

We slept in the car that night; thank God we had a sanctuary. Later we learned from a park ranger that they were biting midges, "no-see-ums" as they were known locally; a type of fly from the Ceratopogonidae family of which there are more than five thousand species around the world. Interesting fact about no-see-ums: like mosquitos, only the females require a blood meal for egg laying; also, they are one of only two pollinators for the cocoa tree. They were so tiny they could easily pass through our netting, like the dust at our camp in California. And they must have had teeth ten times the size of their body, evidenced by the splotches of blood behind our ears.

And so, we continued on our journey, but for me, this adventure was already over. Even though we had the luxury of instant transportation, it hardly made life any easier. We were suffering from an angst that simply rises out of this directionless meander—there are no safety nets. We lived nowhere other than right here, right now, tooling down this lonesome road. We had traveled so far and seen so much that every place looked like every other place in terms of *where do you stop?* America is homogenized, and since everywhere seemed the same, I suppose we could have stopped anywhere. I felt like the sleepwalking character in a Max Fleischer cartoon who, high up in the air, steps from one moving girder to another, miraculously coming to no harm as long as they're asleep. I was anxious to stop, to *wake up* so to speak, and start painting again. I felt like I belonged in a studio somewhere and that riding this endless carousel was a damned waste of time. I didn't know what it was going to take to move into a more natural life, a life that I wanted to live and not this hoboing around the country. I found myself throwing the *I Ching* more often. "How do we know where or when to stop?" I asked. It was a repetitive question since we already received an answer concerning Ithaca, or at least for me it was; Jewell had yet to be convinced. Here was the answer: *K'un / The Receptive. K'un* is the yin in the yin/yang symbol; the receptive, the earth. It's also devotional and responsive to yang, the creative. The description made me think there would be no quick and easy remedy for our current situation, that I needed forbearance and patience in the face of things. It also mentions finding friends (again) that would guide you through your toil and effort; one must forego the act of leading and allow oneself to be lead. The first two lines had movement and carried the stark warning that signs of death and decay, if ignored, would multiply, paving the way for ultimate failure. These lines changed and pointed to the hexagram *Lin/Approach*. It "points to a time of joyous, hopeful progress." But this moment won't last forever so…best to strike when the iron is hot. It seemed the *I Ching* was suggesting that a stop would need to happen soon. For me, this underlined the destination of Ithaca. After such a positive experience there, I had my heart set on returning; all I could think of was going back and leaving this nightmare behind.

We took many twists and turns on the backroads of New England, headed for Bangor, Maine. The forests of Vermont are very rich: crimson-barked evergreens lining the road with occasional strokes of purple lupine undulating as we passed by in our speeding car; the Green Mountains appearing and disappearing continuously in the background. We camped once more before our final assault to the sea. The land was becoming rugged and mountainous as we pierced the northern end of the Appalachians. I didn't know Maine had mountains. The next day we entered Bangor and then circled back down on Highway 1 alongside the Penobscot River. Bangor is at the end of a long crack of river that widens as it empties into the Atlantic. It was great to finally see the ocean but there was something about it that was not as inviting as the Pacific. The Atlantic, at least that day, was cold and gray— ironically claustrophobic in its great expanse, much like the desert in that way. It was the ocean of industry and the look-back of a people released from their past; they could expect no return to their native land. A red sun rises here, over a cast-iron sea, to signify the start of a working day. The Pacific, on the other hand, was the ocean of sunsets and release. A sunset on the Pacific is otherworldly. And it's big enough to almost submerge the volcanic mountains of Hawaii that are taller than the Himalayas when measured from their base. For me, the Pacific expressed that infinity of space and possibility while the Atlantic was more of a barrier, a wall.

I swore I would pick up any and all hitchhikers along the way but, strangely, there was only one; a guy from up the coast. At least, that's what I think he said. I really had trouble understanding his accent. He had a very guttural brogue, like he was trying to talk while swallowing a fish.

"Hey, so where you headed?"

"Belfahst."

"Belfast, huh…how far ahead is that?"

"Not fah. Jus' pas' Shearspoaht."

"Sheerspot? Shearspat?"

"I think he said Searsport," said Jewell, who pulled out a map.

"Yeh, Sshearspoaht. Belfahst izhjes' th' uthuh sshawide uh th' stayt pahk."

"There's a Moose Point State Park he's referring to…just the other side…forthwith," said the navigator with the map.

"Man, I'm sorry, that's quite an accent you have there. Are you…from Maine?"

"Oh, yeh." He laughed. "Ahm a Downeastah fum up neah th' fuckin' Canucks."

He was a "Downeaster" from up near the Canadian border. He reminded me of the blokes who picked us up a year ago at Kakabeka Falls at the start of our journey, only the accent was a lot rougher. We dropped him in "Belfahst" and continued down U.S. Highway 1, apparently the longest north-south numbered road in the country, running from Key West all the way up to Fort Kent, Maine. Our trip was bookended by two highways numbered 1. Somewhere after Freeport we left the highway and scuttled back across a multitude of roads crisscrossing New Hampshire and Vermont to Upstate New York. We had made it to Bangor and back in four days. I did more driving coming back than I did going out there—I just wanted to get off the road and change the direction of my life as soon as possible. I had no idea of what or how I was going to do this, but once we got back, I was prepared to go on welfare. I wasn't going to go through that naked turmoil of having no resources again like when we landed in Berkeley. Isn't that what the system is for, to keep people from slipping through the cracks? I would find out. This odyssey was coming to an end, and we were sailing home in our red rusted barque. Perhaps it would prove to be, as Homer put it, *"a rugged isle, but a good nurse of young men."*

Ithaca

We camped in Buttermilk Falls State Park, just south of the city. Within a week we found a basement apartment, the downstairs portion of a yellow and turquoise house located on the edge of town. The price was a little high but doable. The landlord was a Black Baptist preacher named Tony. I supposed the rent was a little higher than usual because Tony had half a dozen mouths to feed. It was really a mess and needed a lot of cleaning and painting. When it rained, it poured right into the kitchen. Tony brought his boys over to fix the roof and it still poured in; water browned from dissolved kitchen smoke and grease eroded the floor tiles. There were brown mice that lived in the living room, gray mice that lived in the closet, a vole that made a single appearance from under the kitchen cabinets, and a marmot that lived under the porch. There was also a louder *something*, and its family, scrambling and cussing inside the one wall that lay below ground level. I didn't mind; it was home, for now, and we could live with it. And I liked Tony; he never asked if we were employed. There was a small creek next to the house, a quince tree, and lots of flowering wild plants in the vacant land surrounding us. I kept my promise of collecting weeds, pressing and identifying them; after surviving the desert I could never take plants, or water, for granted. Strange thing: one of our early purchases was a used TV and the moment I turned it on I saw a news report about a bunch of folks in wheelchairs taking over the administrative offices in a government building in San Francisco. They were protesting the lack of accommodating infrastructure for the disabled in the Bay Area. The protestors were from CIL, the group we worked for, and there in the middle of it all, leading the charge, was my employer—the one for whom I performed attendant care!

We immediately went on welfare and received two hundred twenty-eight dollars a month plus food stamps and Medicare. It basically paid the rent with a little extra left over for gas and other expenses. It was more than we ever made in California. And we got married. It was the 28th of June, 1976, by a Justice of the Peace. We explained to Jewell's parents that we weren't returning to Minnesota and tried to smooth their feathers. The bride wore black; it was a good joke at the time but as the old Irish saying goes: marry in black, wish you were back (presumably unmarried). The groom wore a white shirt tucked into beltless pants, sandals, and a straw hat. We both had corsages that were later attached to my hat. Our welfare worker was our witness and photographer. Most of our relatives sent gifts. My old friend Billy from Duluth, with whom I had entrusted my record collection ("Don't worry, they'll be safe,") shipped them to me as a wedding present. I was missing about a dozen records. Even my mother sent something: our wedding announcement that we had sent her, stuck inside a candle she had made with some plastic flowers—all of this paraphernalia encased within wax. You could read the announcement through the wax and I noticed that the paper edge of it was burnt. I believe this was simply a decorative device and yet there was something rather funerary about it. My mother was a very complicated woman. The only relatives who didn't send gifts, or even a congratulatory card, were those from Elroy's side of the family. I learned that they refused to recognize the marriage because it was performed in a civic hall and not in a church. It was just another insult doled out from people with a punitive lifestyle. I wondered if they would have recognized our marriage if it had taken place in a synagogue. But Jewell's family was happy, especially her father who was no longer the ogre; I actually started to like him. We finally resembled stability.

Welfare was no picnic. Each week we had to go in and talk to an agent about how our employment search was going. There were postings along the wall and you were supposed to pick one out and get excited about working for fast food restaurants and whatnot. At some point I had to go down to the office, sit with a group of recipients, and be told that we were going to be put into a "volunteer" work situation to work off our "debt." I wondered how we were supposed to find a job if we were volunteering our time all day. We were given an ultimatum, a "if you don't cooperate…" lecture, which was demeaning. Some of the folks running this office were downright hostile and none of them made any sense.

One hot morning in early summer I went down to the Social Services Department to peruse the job listings and pick up my welfare check. I was called to the desk of a rather rotund and bald-headed agent in a white shirt and bow tie, with soaked armpits, who pulled out a piece of paper from the pile on his desk and said, "Here's a job for you at the hospital: picking up bodies from beds."

"I'd rather not," I said.

"You're refusing to apply for this job?"

"I'm looking for library work, or something similar," I said. "I have a bad back; I can't be lifting bodies like that all day."

He stared at me. "Are you telling me you're not willing to take this job?"

"Uhm…well, yeah, I can't do it."

"All right, then. Be seated. You will be called."

I went back to one of the metal folding chairs lined up against the wall. I didn't know what to think; why was I being offered a nurse's aide job when, clearly, I had filled out the forms indicating my experience as a librarian's assistant. I thought maybe they were looking at my last job as an attendant care person, which I had only done for a few months, and had stuck me in the wrong category. And after crisscrossing the country with a heavy pack, the last thing I wanted to be doing all day was lift dead weight. Suddenly my name was called. I thought, "Do they have something else for me?" Nope. They handed me my check and I was free to go.

The next day I received a letter stating that my welfare funds were canceled, including food stamps and Medicare, because I refused work. I was naive enough to believe that welfare would help me find meaningful work. That bastard never gave me a warning. He reminded me of the border guard who arrested us coming into Canada the previous year. The "Kozmic Trooth" I learned from life on the road would be the same for the road of life: life is a series of circles and here I was again being done in by another petty asshole. I called up the agency to explain but they didn't care. A hearing was not even offered. Their job was to get people off welfare any way they could—not keep them on. And so I found out that, yes, you can slip through the cracks; the system doesn't care. Social Services is not an employment agency. I was once again strolling through the ruins of desperation. My only hope was pinned to a job at the Tompkins County Public Library where I had applied for a part-time position a week earlier. But how tough could the competition be? My only work experience, besides the attendant care-person gig in Berkeley, was a few years of library work when a student. I decided it was time for another ritual, like that "letter to the world" I had written and posted to a tree in Berkeley. But this time it would not be a letter. Instead, it would be a gesture. I had visited the Herbert F. Johnson Museum of Art, located on the Cornell campus, where I saw an old wooden sculpture of a seated Buddha on display. So, in an impromptu mood I picked a rose from someone's garden, snuck it into the museum beneath my shirt, and placed it behind the statue as an offering. I stood there praying silently for that job at the library. The next day I got the job. I was in competition with around forty other applicants; *somebody up there likes me*.

Still, all was not well. To further mess things up, I received another letter from Public Assistance saying that now half my wages from the library would be put towards Jewell's welfare check. In other words, together we would be making less than if I had stayed unemployed since my part-time paycheck was not that much. Together we wouldn't make enough to support ourselves, so the only thing to do was to get completely free of the dole. Jewell was able to do that by landing a part-time job at a hospital not too far from the house. We were on public assistance for about three months.

With the hassles of welfare behind us, life was becoming more routine and less haphazard. We were poor but resembled something closer to what one may consider normal. I was beginning to feel more settled in life and not so much of an outcast. I discovered that marriage had a very beneficial effect; I was happy with domesticity and didn't know I could feel this way. I wasn't as wild as I had been, only a year earlier, rambling along on the road. In short, I was more of a square than I thought. But hitchhiking taught me that, if you don't like where you are, you can just get up and move under your own power and find new options. It will change you, but your core remains the same. Don't be afraid to toss yourself out into space—you will land on your feet. My "searching" was now relegated towards creativity and intellectual pursuits. Our relationship changed, ever so slightly. Jewell seemed softer to me and more caring. We were the young married couple.

I bought some art materials for painting, picked up where I'd left off from my days in the Richmond studio, and made some large canvases measuring roughly five feet by six feet. Our tiny basement apartment could hardly accommodate them so I'd stretch and then remove them, one at a time, from the same stretcher frame. One of these paintings had a black and yellow diagonal striped image running through the middle of it; road signage for "Hazard" or "Caution" that I had seen so many times while hitchhiking. Jewell had the spare bedroom for her writing and, curiously, her sewing and quilt making apparatus. I say curiously because she was into these traditional women's crafts as a vehicle for "making it new" (to misquote Pound). I suppose, like Judy Chicago, Jewell was exploring women's traditions from a feminist angle. And she thought of her writing as being akin to sewing; a stitching of repeated words influenced by both Gertrude Stein and concrete poetry.

Culturally, we were blessed in having an Ivy League school nearby. Carl Sagan ran the astronomy department and gave his annual lecture to the public in Cornell's auditorium. Pete Seeger came and played at the same auditorium. Stan Brakhage, the famous underground filmmaker, gave a lecture in a small classroom (I could hardly comprehend him). At another time, Sagan gave a screening of a 1945 movie in an intimate and rather old and moldy smelling theater located in one of the campus buildings. He said that the film we were about to watch had influenced him, when he was a boy, for his later interest in physics. Before the movie began, Sagan introduced us to another fellow there who was known for being a proponent of a theory wherein the universe would eventually stop expanding and reverse itself to an infinitely tiny point once again, fulminating in another Big Bang. The movie was "Dead of Night" and has a circular narrative—the beginning is also the ending of the story.

Vito Acconci, an art hero of mine, came to the art museum on campus and gave a three-day lecture. Vito was famous for what was known as "Body Art" back in the late 1960s. His work was subversive and often confrontational. I was lucky enough to have been standing in the museum when he came in. He walked up to me rather directly and asked, "Where's the lecture hall?" Of course, I didn't know. But I experienced a strange aura about the man; an intensity that seemed to emanate from his body so that, should he turn and talk to someone else, you would be left in the absence of his energy. He was like the revolving light in a lighthouse. It was very weird—first he's directing all his energy at you and then, all of a sudden, it's not there. Each day the lectured audience became smaller until the third day when there were only a dozen or so of us sitting at a long and intimate table with him. Everyone theorized about the nature and future of art. Vito wore camouflage clothing, like a foot soldier from the trenches, and was constantly fidgeting with cigarettes; smoking them, putting them out, lighting them up and tossing them scattershot to the floor's warzone beneath his chair.

I began writing to Mom and Elroy. I never wrote them while in California. Like the burnt wedding announcement, my mother's letters were filled with mixed messages difficult to comprehend. They were gamey, cryptic and full of hidden malice. And yet, on the surface, they seemed quite pleasant. But I knew that something was brewing beneath those clouds of civility. For the first time, neither one of them had any control over me. And since they couldn't employ their usual one-upmanship anymore, they were at a loss as to how to relate. They were eerily too polite—to the point of phoniness. My mother's cutesy way of getting under my skin was no longer effective. Jewell's theory at the beginning of our journey that our parents would come around sooner or later because that's how families are was not going to be happening for my little group. And I didn't think it would. I was just happy to be hundreds of miles away from this poison.

Eventually, Jewell and I found jobs at Cornell. I left the public library after a year or so and worked at the Uris Library on campus. Jewell found a job in the Office of Alumni Affairs. We moved into a much nicer and cheaper apartment. Our new landlord was a Sicilian gentleman who was thought to be one hundred and three years old. His family didn't keep track; each year he liked to celebrate his ninety-ninth birthday. I can still see him, out in his backyard, against a small forest, tossing scraps of meat and fat to a murder of hungry crows.

We were happy for a little while with our new apartment and new jobs, and had acquired a few friends, but I could tell Jewell was getting restless again. I could feel these dark maneuverings going on beneath her brow; similar seismic perturbations akin to the California exodus, which would manifest in an incomprehensible indifference towards me. Finally, she said, "You know, we can't live here forever."

Uh-oh, now what? I thought.

"I think we need to go back to school and finish our degrees," she said.

She was right about that. Ithaca was a lovely place to rest but, after a couple of years, it can turn to stagnation. I could have stagnated a little longer, but Jewell was quite adamant about moving on and making a future for ourselves by going back to school.

We began looking at our options. Jewell wanted to return to Minnesota, something she knew I did not want to do; I wanted to be as far away from my parents as possible. She flew home to visit her folks and meet with my old professor, Phil Meany, someone she had also admired, to get his advice. I was happy to hear he didn't think moving back was a good idea; that it was a step backwards to come "home." And so, we applied to different places in New York and ended up being accepted at the S.U.N.Y. College at Purchase, a perfect place for an art major. Jewell would major in English and didn't care where we went. The school had one of the best art making facilities in the state as well as a Performing Arts Center, Film School, and more. The Neuberger Museum of Art, a major institution housing modern, contemporary and African works, is also located on campus. The master architects of the campus included Philip Johnson and John Burgee and was founded by Governor Nelson Rockefeller who touted it as the "cultural gem of the SUNY system." The Art Department had state of the art print shops; lithography, etching, serigraphy, you name it. Most universities fund their art department last, if at all, and I was happy to find a school that valued the arts. We would try to save some money for the big move in a year.

Meanwhile, I made the acquaintance of an art historian, a professor from the Art History Department at Cornell. I told her I was an artist and she said that her department had a gallery; if I dropped off my slides, she'd have a look and maybe I could get a show there. I got busy making some horrible slides and dropped them off with her secretary. To my surprise, in a couple of weeks I was offered their exhibition space. Of course, I knew very few people at the time, and so there was no opening or fanfare. She wanted me to come to her class and talk to her students but I was too shy and declined the offer. Being a searcher didn't mean you had all the answers, in fact all you really have are questions. I was too young and felt too green. But still, having that show was confidence-building, just to know that someone valued what you did. A one-man show at an Ivy League school—what could be better than that for someone in their early twenties?

Another great thing about working at Cornell was that Jewell had access to a plethora of phone books in her office.

One day she said to me, "You know, whenever you talk about your folks, you always refer to your dad as '*my* dad.'"

"What do you mean?"

"Well, I almost never say *my* dad. I just say Dad."

"Yeah, so?"

"So you keep saying '*my* dad' this, and '*my* dad' that, but he's not your real father, and it always struck me as peculiar that you preface 'Dad' with '*my*.'"

"What's your point?" It was true, I had never thought about how I spoke of Elroy. My mother was always referring to him as "*your* dad" so I naturally extended that title when talking about him.

"Have you ever thought of looking up your real father, George Grandbouche? And, you know, maybe get in touch with him?"

"How?"

"I have access to just about any phonebook in the country. I'll go through them and look up 'Grandbouche' if you like."

"Let me think about it."

"Sure; whenever you feel like it. As long as I'm working there we'll have access."

With a name like Grandbouche I knew there wouldn't be that many to find and that my father should be fairly easy to track down. But I was very conflicted as to whether or not I should inform Mom and Elroy of these developments. On the one hand, we had just resumed communications and progress towards a détente could be thwarted. On the other, if one is to have an honest relationship then everything should be out in the open and on the table. If I kept silent, I would be playing the same coy games my mother often played with me, which I hated. I didn't want the burden of stealth on my end—better to live free and in the open. I decided to throw an *I Ching*. The results were the first hexagram, "Ch'ien / The Creative" with a changing line at the bottom, a nine; this changing line gave further commentary in hexagram 44, "Kou, Coming to Meet." The unbroken lines of the first hexagram represents the light, it has a primal power, is strong and active, and "without weakness." It also represents the creative force of nature and the spiritual essence in man. Being the first hexagram, it is very important and there are quite a few pages dedicated to its description. But what got me was the changing line at the beginning, that nine that breaks it and changes it to hexagram 44. The nine at the beginning means: "Hidden dragon. Do not act." I was floored. The *I Ching* was telling me not to act. Moreover, hexagram 44, "Coming to Meet," had an image of darkness rising and penetrating the light. Symbolically, the image is that of an innocent looking girl who surrenders herself to a powerful figure and thus seizes power. So, this further comment was telling me that, if I did decide to try and find my real father, I should resist the temptation (the girl symbol) of telling Mom and Elroy. And so, I would. For now. Who knows? Maybe things will change. I gave Jewell the go-ahead and sure enough she eventually found a George Grandbouche, living in Arizona. I wrote to this address and got a reply from my grandmother Leata whom I had never met (as an adult). She was happy to hear from me and forwarded my letter on to her son, who lived in Grand Junction, Colorado, George Grandbouche, Jr. Sadly, George Senior, my grandfather, had passed away a few years earlier and that was who Jewell had located. I was christened George III. George sent us tickets and we were on our way to Colorado. I was twenty-five years old when I finally met my father.

George

I didn't know what to expect after hearing all those awful stories about my father but it turned out to be a truly amazing experience. Walking into the terminal, I recognized him right away from the photos my mother and grandmother had. But I also had a clear memory of him from when I was an infant. We hugged and I could feel his thin frame echoing my own, a pack of Tiparillos stuck in his breast pocket. Seeing him again—for the first time—was the opening of a great primordial mystery. Barb, his wife, came forward and gave us a hug. She pointed to a large patch of frosted skin on his chin, a runaway herpes wound, and said, "He's been so nervous about meeting you he got this." His three kids came up to us as well, Jay, Scott, and Todd, all boys. The family joke was that the Grandbouches never had girls so they had to go out and find their own. If I had had a kid, I'm sure I would have had a son too.

Back at their house I met George's mom, my grandmother Leata, the one to whom I had written. She lived a stone's throw away from the house in a trailer parked next to their peach orchard. She was very sweet and endearing and quite unflappable. She had lived most of her life in Iowa, a place that she missed, and had a pragmatic sense of things that growing up on a farm engenders.

When we walked inside the house, I saw an old photo of me when I was three years old, one that I was quite familiar with, hanging on the wall with all their other family photos. George said he would point the picture out to his boys and say, "He's going to look me up some day." But if not for Jewell, I don't know how long that may have taken. I was only three at the time of the divorce and my mother had very nearly achieved wiping him out of my mind. I had a lot of questions that I thought I might finally get some answers to, or at least hear the other side of the story. George took me into his office and pulled out a file.

"Here you go," he said.

"What's this?"

"Grandbouche vs Grandbouche."

"Ah...the divorce."

"Yep. Some letters too."

He had kept all those letters that he'd received from my mother, and they were quite revealing. I saw more photos of myself, as a four- or five-year-old, digging in the garden or playing in the yard, with cutesy captions written on them. My mother had tried to entice him back to Davenport by using pictures of me as bait. After listening for years to all the disdain and pent-up anger she felt towards George, I was a bit shocked at these letters of entreaty.

"So what happened? Why'd you guys get divorced?" I asked.

"Your mother was always flying back home every time I went out into the field. I'd come home to an empty house, and after a while, I couldn't take it anymore. Sometimes she'd be gone for a month, staying with her mother in Rock Island. I gave her an ultimatum: you go again, you stay. And that's what she did."

"So...you didn't desert her then..." I said.

"She deserted me!"

This was a revelation. No one, none of my relatives, had ever heard the real reason for the split. The stories my mother told about George being a womanizer and wanting to get rid of her so he could marry the boss's daughter was all a big lie. Not even Elroy knew the truth. Now I understood what all that traveling was about. "Believe it or not I remember lots of trains and planes," I said.

"Really?" He laughed. "You remember all that back and forth, huh?"

"Yep...so you didn't marry the boss's daughter?" It was an embarrassing question, but I had to ask.

"Ha! Is that what she told you?"

"Nah...I heard it...around," I said, remembering what Grandma Genny had told me.

"No. I met Barb at a divorcee party. There were a bunch of us getting divorced and we all had the same lawyer. We'd meet at his office in Moab and then later go out for some drinks," he laughed.

"How come you didn't visit me?" I asked.

"I tried to get you for the summers. She wouldn't allow it. And anyway, you were too far away. It wasn't easy for me to drop everything and come get you, not to mention interstate custody laws back then. I sent you toys instead."

"I remember them...they were really great; my favorites."

George smiled.

I could see that being adopted by Elroy was so unnecessary. I began to realize it must have been my mother's idea to do that so she could get even with George for having been dumped. I was used as bait, and when that didn't work, I was used as a weapon. All those lost years, and for what? My mother was very tyrannical, someone who always needed to win a perceived battle. Perhaps her marriage to Elroy was nothing more than a convenience; the move of a chess piece. And likewise, Elroy's interest in my mother was a convenience; the pretty girl who lived next door. Neither of them had the wherewithal, or imagination, to look very far. I don't think she ever truly got over George. Maybe it didn't help that I began to look like him as I grew older. And it wasn't just the physical resemblance we shared; there was also a certain expansiveness to his character that I could recognize in myself. He had the spirit of an adventurer and so did I. My three younger brothers had this same spirit and a love for the wide-open spaces: living expressions of the Wild West. It was no wonder my mother made such a fuss whenever I asserted myself, telling me I was, "acting just like George."

I asked her once why I was called by my middle name rather than my first and her reply was that she was so hurt by him that she didn't want to be reminded of the past. I told George this and he laughed.

"Oh, that's balderdash. We started calling you Rollie because every time someone called for George, three people would look up."

After getting to know George a little better I began to wonder how my parents ever became entangled. George loved roughing it in the great outdoors whereas Mom was a homebody. George loved to gamble on an adventure; Mom easily became homesick. Mom was, at that time, a devout Catholic; George, an agnostic. He never went to church but she had to go no matter what or where or how inconvenient. George, and all the rest of his family, thought she was crazy.

After their marriage, my father attended the University of Wisconsin at Madison and graduated with a degree in Mining Engineering. I was born at General Hospital, which no longer exists. It's now called the Medical Sciences Center on the UW campus—perhaps the nursery is now a laboratory.

After graduating, George was in need of a job and came out to Grand Junction, with my mother and me, to visit a friend who worked for the nascent Atomic Energy Commission, later known as the Department of Energy. They needed mining engineers and so George applied and found a new life for us, much to my mother's consternation. She thought she was simply on a vacation. Mom was not happy being uprooted, nor in having to join an army of mining engineers and their families at various campsites sprinkled throughout the deserts of the Western States.

George's job at the AEC was to locate uranium, mark it on a map, and then release those maps to private industry and individual prospectors. After a couple of years he quit the AEC and went into the consulting business, which is how we ended up in Moab. This tiny town, which consisted of two or three graveled streets, experienced a uranium boom in the 1950s and became known as the "Uranium Capital of the World" after a geologist named Charlie Steen struck it rich not too far from the city. It was like the gold rush of the previous century with prospectors rushing in, hoping to find those copious veins that could make them overnight millionaires.

The material that made the atom bomb was being gouged out of the earth at a prodigious rate due to the mid-century madness of cold war politics. The government wanted to feel secure in the knowledge that it had enough ore for making atomic bombs.

George took Jewell and me over to where he worked, the Department of Energy's Grand Junction Projects Office, and showed us around. He had returned to working for the government and was in charge of land leases for the mining of uranium by utility companies, cleaning up the mill tailings they left behind.

He pointed to a huge pile of rocks outside his office window and said, "You see that? Those are tailings from the Manhattan Project."

"Are they still radioactive?" Jewell asked.

"You bet." he said.

"That's horrible," I said.

"Aw, a little radioactivity isn't going to hurt you."

I was appalled. "How can you say that?"

"Look, you get about as much radiation from the sun as you would from that pile out there. Nothin' to it."

As it turned out, the downtown sidewalks in Grand Junction are also filled with uranium mill tailings, as are countless buildings—any place where concrete was poured. I joked that it must be giving the bottom of your feet a lovely tan as you shop for sandals. I couldn't believe he was so *laissez-faire* about radioactivity. I guess he was ensconced, like many others of his generation and/or livelihood, in the romance of the Atomic Age. That night we were all having drinks around the pool table when he handed me a Geiger counter.

"Now you take this thing out to that shed there and see if you can locate some prime ore I have. Don't worry it's in a lead box. But don't turn the light on...see if you can find it in the dark."

It wasn't hard to do. I stumbled around drunk, holding the probe like a seasoned dowser, and found it quite easily. Even in a lidless lead box that thing was throwing out invisible sparks that made the device sound like a sputtering mini-bike.

When I came back to the house, there was a lively conversation going on about our hitchhiking adventures.

"Did'ja find some uranium?" George quipped.

"Sure did…glad it's in a lead box…I think."

Everyone laughed. Jewell had mentioned our weird ride across the Mojave and getting stuck in Las Vegas.

"Yeah, we couldn't get a ride out of there," I said. "So we had to fly out. I remember looking out the window and thought I saw a crater."

"You probably did," George said. "The Sedan Crater is out there—about ninety miles from Las Vegas. Or it's possible you saw another one; that whole area is pockmarked with nuclear test craters. I witnessed one of them. You could see the earth ripple and move like a wave coming towards you from ground zero and then, bump, pass right under you. It was scary."

Early the next day, our tribe loaded up the RV and we headed south to Telluride. We went camping for a few days at Woods Lake, an incredibly beautiful area; stately aspens surrounding a picture-postcard lake. We all got to know each other a little better. Growing up an only child, it was odd to suddenly have all these siblings; they felt more like long lost cousins. Everyone kept asking me if I thought the West was better than the East. They had me stereotyped—as if I were some sort of city slicker. Hell, I lived in a rural area of New York, and anyway, I'm from the Midwest. That didn't seem to matter. Finally, I asked Jay what he considered "East" and his reply was, "Anything east of the Rockies!" I never felt more at home than with these people.

Grandma Leata had also come along on the trip and we got to talking one night around the campfire about my mother. She told me that she had noticed I was always by myself in my room, and so she had asked her why I wasn't playing outside on such a beautiful day. My mother's reply was, "You think he's got it bad? I had nowhere to play but in the attic!" Besides offering insight to my mother's lunacy that also explained why I didn't have any friends until I was in third grade. I remembered the traumatic stories my mother told of being abused by her grandmother. Later I learned that the attic was where my mother could escape from the grandmother. And so, the beat goes on.

After the camping trip, and with only a day or two left of our visit, George asked if there was anything we'd like to do before going back. I asked, "How far is Moab?"

"Moab? It's less than two hours from here."

"Could we possibly go there?"

"You want to see the old place?" he asked.

"Yeah, if it's not too much trouble."

"No trouble at all. Let's just go by ourselves, though— you, me, and Jewell."

And so off we went for the day. On the way out of town, George pointed to the Book Cliffs that swoop down into Grand Junction, and all the exposed geological stratifications of nearby mountains dissolved in the acid of time. Eventually we came to the deserts of Utah and George picked out areas by the roadside that he said were once towns. All you could see were blips in the whitewashed plains of this great expanse, with a streak of rail from an abandoned train route here and there hidden beneath the sand—detritus from eroding mountains. I thought of our hitchhiking through the Mojave and how lucky we were to have survived it.

After about an hour and a half we made the descent into Moab from the north along highway 191. At first, everything looked the same, but just as we rounded the corner near Arches National Park, the landscape changed dramatically. The intense redness of the rock, and the anticipation of what lay ahead, made me think of Rachmaninoff's "Isle of the Dead." It would be the perfect musical score for entering this majestic valley. George had a lot to say, from a geologist's perspective, about the eroded rock formations that greet the visitor to this corner of the Earth. But, for me, these citadel walls were a gigantic relief sculpture resembling the Konark Sun Temple of the Hindus, and spoke as if in a dream of lost myths from an unknown people. The thought occurred to me that, if you were mad enough, you'd be able to read the narrative of the images in the rocks. I tossed this idea to George who said, "Well, you're not too far off the beam. There are Indian petroglyphs all over the place. There's even a whole slew of them not too far from the road called Newspaper Rock about an hour to the south.

"Why do they call it Newspaper Rock?" Jewell asked.

"Because there are hundreds of petroglyphs carved into the rock; it looks like a newspaper."

214

"Cool. Can we go see them?" I asked.

"You bet. Here's something up ahead though that we can see right away."

He pulled over to a parking area just north of the Colorado River. We got out and stretched our legs in the mid-morning sun. A profound silence enveloped us. We walked up a path towards the canyon wall, flanked by an arroyo, through scruffy tufts of desert grass until we reached an area of rock that was covered in spiritual images.

"What in the world is this?" I was blown away.

"This here's the 'Courthouse Wash Rock,'" George said.

"So these are called petroglyphs?" Jewell asked.

"These are actually petrograms. They're painted instead of scratched into the rock. And they're a lot rarer and harder to get to...except for this one."

"Wow, I can't believe it," I said. "So how'd they paint that? Who painted it? How old is it?"

"These are between fifteen hundred and four thousand years old. They're painted using ground up minerals mixed with animal fat. No one knows who did them or what it means, but look," he pointed down the length of the gallery, "there's a bunch more continuing down towards the gully."

The more you looked, the more you saw. There were hundreds of figures, not as fancy as the ones at the head of the line and all rather plain looking as if a crowd of people simply came to signify their presence at a ritual; an ancient "Kilroy was here." The figures at the extreme right, however, were clearly in charge. I climbed upon the rock that sits in front of these images to get a closer look. One figure had horns and arms that resemble those of a scorpion. Abstract symbols emanating energetically from some of them; others resembled aquatic creatures, dragonflies and insects of some sort. I also noticed that someone had taken a potshot at this national treasure. There were bullet holes pockmarking it here and there made by just another gun-toting asshole. After the rock art, we drove across the muddy Colorado into Moab for a look at the old house. It was an ochre-brick mid-century modern dwelling not too far from Main Street. A huge air conditioner sat upon its flat roof.

"Well, there it is," said George.

"Wow. Believe it or not, I actually remember this," I said.

"Let's see if they'll let us take a look around," said George.

We walked up to the door and rang the bell. An elderly man swung the door open; his wife approached from behind.

"Hi," George said. "You know, I was the first owner of this house and my son here was just a baby then and hasn't seen it for all these years and I was wondering if you folks wouldn't mind if we just took a quick peek inside?"

"Sure, come right in. Where you folks from?"

"Oh, I'm livin' in Grand Junction now," said George. "These folks are visiting from out east." We smiled and looked around. I remembered all of it: the hallway to the bedrooms, the kitchen, and the picture window with a view of the red hills that surround Moab.

George whispered to me, "Take a good look at that hall; I'll tell you about it later."

216

Pleasantries passed freely and then we left. Jewell took a picture of me in front of the house wearing a cowboy hat of George's that I seemed to have coveted.

"What about the hall?" I asked.

"That's where your mother used to have her fits and throw pots and pans at me!" George laughed.

"Jesus. What did you do?"

"Hell if I know; I don't remember now. But it didn't take much."

The thought of my mother throwing things at someone was strange; I'd never seen her get that angry. But in a way it didn't surprise me. It was comic and sad at the same time; just another cliché she thought she had to enact after seeing it in a movie.

We found a little place for lunch on Main Street that served Mexican food and planned our next move over fajitas, tacos, and enchiladas.

"You know it might be getting too late for that drive down to Newspaper Rock," I said, stuffing my mouth with another taco.

"You're probably right," George said. "But there's always next time, right?"

"They say you should always leave something undone so you'll come back," said Jewell.

"I like that," said George. "Well, there's more stuff to see right here near town anyway."

George picked up the tab and ushered us out into the sun-drenched street and the heat of the car. "I know a place that

217

has more petroglyphs and something else you oughta see," he said. We headed back to the north, crossing the Colorado, and then took a quick turn to the left. We pulled off a few miles down a road that runs parallel to the river and parked in a graveled lot. "It's up here," he said. We followed him up a trail, lizards scattering at our dusty footfall, until we reached the end and came to a beautiful view of the river valley. The rusted walls of the striated Entrada Sandstone reached down to the river across the way, bearded in tamarisk.

"Beautiful," I said.

"Not that, this!" he said, pointing up towards a ledge behind us.

"What, another damn rock?" I joked.

"Look a little closer," he said. I looked. I stared. And then I saw it: a claw mark sunk into the rock, and then another, maybe three or four feet away, going in the same direction. Here was a three-toed dinosaur track left by an animal that was running across a mud flat at least seventy million years ago. It was probably the size of an ostrich.

"Oh look, there's more," Jewell said, pointing to another, smaller, track to the left. Every little dent in that ledge of rock came alive, revealing the incidence of formation.

"Seeing this, it's really not hard to imagine these things running around," I said. "It's almost like it just happened yesterday."

George chuckled. "That was quite a few yesterdays ago."

We backtracked down the trail and found some petroglyphs: images of bighorn sheep being hunted by stick

218

figures holding bows and arrows. The figures were not as old as the painted ones of the Courthouse Wash; these were only a few hundred years or less. They were less abstract and easier to comprehend. Or were they? Obviously it was some sort of communication and had a familiarity about it, like language. On the surface you see the hunt, but what was the purpose of showing this? To tell of good hunting in the area? Or is there a reason for the archer pointing in that particular direction? And is he pointing at the sheep or the larger figure wearing a headdress, holding a shield and spear? Maybe it's a war. Why is one sheep bigger than the hunter; and what about that strange water-bug creature standing as tall as the man? And what makes you think these images were all made at the same time, giving only the illusion of communication. Or is language itself an illusion; something that is ephemeral, in transit, and of the moment; breaking down over time. I decided that this rather pedestrian type of image making was a lot more complicated than it first appeared. We don't know if there were bighorn sheep in this area; maybe the sheep were just symbols. You couldn't take it at face value. It may not be about a hunt at all.

The sun was attenuating its hold on the day, a warm yellow light casting blue shadows that approached our own height. "Well, we should probably start heading back," George said.

Along the way I talked about that memory I had of being drunk when I was two or three, twirling about in the muddy banks of a river, and looking up at the stars.

"Oh, that wouldn't be the first time you were trying to take a nip," he said. "We caught you once taking a sip straight out of a bottle of scotch when we were having a picnic. You had just started walking. We all thought it was pretty funny."

"Where was that muddy place though, do you remember?" I asked.

"I think I know what you're talking about. It was right along here on the Colorado. I'll take you there; it's on the way home."

We took a different route back, Highway 128, a scenic shortcut that snakes along with the river to Cisco and back to Interstate 70. The drive was magnificent. I could see why the surrealist Max Ernst loved the American South West. His painting, "Petrified City," loomed around every corner.

Eventually we came to a bridge that crosses the river. George pulled over and we walked down to the rushing brown water.

"Well, here it is," he said.

"You sure this is it? Sure doesn't look all that familiar," I said.

"Yeah, I couldn't forget *that*; you threw up in the back seat of my brand-new Buick!"

We entered Grand Junction near sunset, a little tired and anxious about having to fly home the next day. After dinner we packed our suitcases and made ready for the early ride out to the airport. Barb, ever the Master of Ceremonies for this family, made sure we had all our stuff in order and ready to go. More of their friends came over to wish us well. It was great to have found this bunch of people and to have been accepted as one of their own. After the company left, I drifted down the hall with George to look at all the framed family photos. I was glad to be alone with him for a moment because there was one more question I had that may have been difficult to answer with a crowd of people around.

"When my mother remarried, why did you agree to the adoption?" I asked.

"In the beginning, I was having trouble with the alimony," he said. "And anyway, the courts favored the mother in custody decisions back then. I'm sorry, I wish things could have been otherwise. But I always knew you'd look me up someday, and here you are."

I wasn't quite sure what to make of this. Although I could understand his intuitive approach to life, I felt that George's take on intuition could easily be mistaken for magical thinking. I was so shut down at the prospect of looking up my real father that, had I not been prodded by Jewell or if she hadn't had access to all those phonebooks, it may have taken many more years before considering such a thing. Of course, it could also be said that if I hadn't thrown an *I Ching* to determine where we would stop, at that precise moment in time, then Jewell wouldn't have had the opportunity to work at Cornell and have access to all those phone books. By using the oracle, and not making a conscious choice, new avenues were opened and presented to me. And ironically, it was my mother who had abandoned me by allowing Elroy, a stranger, to impose his will and brand of discipline upon a child he didn't know and with whom he had only an artificial relationship. I am still not sure I ever got a satisfactory answer to this. But such is life. I'm not sure we ever get a satisfactory answer to a lot of things. Perhaps we shouldn't want them; unfinished paintings have a certain mystery.

We boarded the plane in the morning. I sat by the window and could see George waving from the fence line. I started to tear up a bit…wasn't expecting that. I had no idea how profoundly one could be affected by simply finding one's roots.

We came home to a pile of mail. One of the pieces was a letter from Mother. I answered it right away. And I told her. This was the only time I didn't heed the advice of the *I Ching*. I just didn't care. I had found a whole other family and this was my new life now, take it or leave it. It took her six months to answer and our relationship slowly dissolved over time. The dragon was released. Nothing would ever be the same.

Strangely, the relationship between Jewell and I also began to unravel. We needed to find full-time work now, at least for a year, so we would have enough money to move and go back to school. Jewell went full-time at her job but I was unable to. Working all day in an office was an unfamiliar grind for her, and it would have been for me too, but it was necessary. A sad and lonely child began to inhabit the room; Jewell was the locus of an alien despair that sought to insinuate itself into our world with a simple proclamation:

"I want to be free to have an affair," she said.

"Beg your pardon?"

"I am so tired and bored with this life. I hate my work. I need an escape."

"But...you've got to be kidding," I said.

"What? Is this so difficult to understand? You try working this long."

"No. I know this year is rough. I tried..."

"Yeah, I know you tried to get that opening at the library—and they were shits for hiring from outside. But maybe you can find another job somewhere else. Maybe you can't. It doesn't matter. I want an open marriage."

"You...don't love me anymore?"

"Yes, yes, yes," she cooed soothingly. "I still love you. I just need this for myself."

"No. I don't like this. You're not making any sense," I said.

"Love is unconditional. How can you deny me this?" she asked.

"What am I supposed to do? Be happy for you?"

"Be happy for yourself. You're free to have an affair as well," she said.

The person I thought I knew was gone, just when I was feeling good about marriage and family. As liberal, or hippie-beatnik-bohemian and culturally experimental as I thought I was, I would not be able to meet this development in our relationship. We never should have married. Her endearing comment of how, "We'd be together anyway," made in that hotel room in Seneca Falls was as much of a ruse as telling her parents we were getting married, and by the way, please send money. But, I suppose there are vast spectrums of reasons why people mistakenly get married, confusing love with some other unconscious desire that each fulfills, temporarily and by chance, for the other. At least we knew why we got married: it was to buy a car.

And so, I had found a new family, just when my own was falling apart. I began to feel very alone for the first time in our relationship. We would be alone together. The next few years would be fraught with jealousy, strife, and emotional turmoil.

New York

In a couple of years, we had moved to Port Chester, New York, living a few miles from where we graduated. Our relationship had continued on a steady downward spiral. I was never on board with the idea of an open marriage and quietly tolerated her desire for sexual freedom, hoping that it would pass. She had her flirtations and a fling, and so did I, but only as retaliation. I thought maybe we could just keep on going as we always did and put it all behind us—but there was an undercurrent of animosity from her that, at the time, I was blind to.

Jewell had been writing letters to a fellow poet she admired and decided to go visit him. He lived in another state. I thought it strange but who was I to say no? You can't control another human being. My only concern was that she was being rather callous doing this around Christmas time. She flew down to see him and then got on the phone with me to declare that she was in love, and that we needed a divorce as soon as possible. So here I was, talking to my runaway wife on the phone while watching a flaming Yule Log on a tiny black-and-white TV on Christmas Eve. I couldn't believe it. A phone conversation is no way to break off a marriage—we'd talk some more when she got back.

I went to pick her up, still thinking that perhaps we could get some counseling. She was quite resolute, and very solemn, in the ride back to the house; I was chauffeuring a dark and alien passenger. We got out of the car and had a showdown right there in the driveway.

"I love this man and I'm going to have his children," she said.

My head was spinning. "What are you talking about? You don't even know this guy!"

"I know enough to know that I can't be in this marriage any longer. And anyway, we had a conjugal visit and I'm going to have his baby."

At this, I just broke down. My knees buckled; it was as if the air was literally knocked out of me. "I...huhh... can't... huhh...believe...what...huhh...you're doing...huhh..." I was gasping for air. The brutality of this experience was not unlike the beatings I took as a kid. After all we had been through, and after getting our degrees, she was leaving me for a prison-poet—the guy was in prison for killing his wife. Where's the feminism in that? Why would she throw it all away and what the hell was she getting herself into, marrying some rough character in a prison? This was insanity.

226

I think she took pity on me, seeing me in this hysterical condition. She spoke very soothingly, as if to a child, and said, "Okay, let's go see a marriage counselor. I'll make an appointment tomorrow." I stopped crying. We went into the house and exchanged unwrapped Christmas gifts. It was bitter.

The next morning Jewell dropped me off, as usual, at the train station. I worked in New York City at a professional lithography atelier, a high-end print shop that collaborated with well-known artists making hand-crafted limited editions. When I came home in the evening, she would be there to pick me up. That was the routine. I waited at the station for about an hour and then decided to walk the three miles home. If she was running late, she'd see me walking the only route we took. But when I got home, I discovered Jewell was gone. She had taken the car, with all her belongings; nothing left of her but a "good-bye" note. There would be no appointment with a counselor.

Jewell's "Dear John" letter was a couple of pages, most of which I threw away, but there was one piece that I kept. It said something to the effect that my penchant for nostalgia was so intense that her optimism and perseverance could never balance out our relationship. Oh really? Well, don't piss on my back and tell me it's raining. More likely Jewell felt she had to move on to another "project"—she had an affinity towards, and a need for defending, society's underdogs. That's what was admirable about her. Even though the sentiment of the letter was bullshit, the one sentence that I kept was a nice little piece of drama. So I tore it out and stuck it into a painting as a collage element. The title of the piece was "Death Car." It was exhibited in a Purchase Alumni group show. I later tore it out and threw it away.

After a while I was glad she left. Our mutual jealousies and infidelities of the last three years were finally over. I had a dream at that time: I dreamed I was very old, with long white hair and beard, and that I was pushing out on the back door of the house where we lived, trying to get out, while Jewell, looking very young as when we first met, was on the outside pushing in on the same door. Suddenly the door disappeared, and we were facing each other. She said, "I was too young." Right then everything clicked, and I felt better when I awoke. She *was* too young. But the truth is we were both too young. Love, like life, changes; it was time to move on. There was too much of my own life to be lived. She wrote me letters expressing a similar feeling of how we had simply grown up together and that it was time for a new chapter. Why she kept writing to me though I have no idea; I guess she was still looking to me for support—an old habit. She wanted to stay in touch but the only way for me to get through a pain like this is to break free. I found a do-it-yourself divorce kit in the want ads of the *Village Voice* for a hundred and twenty dollars. Thank God we didn't have kids, or it would have been more complicated.

I should also add that her decision to leave occurred after her father died. Now that the Omnipotent Father was deceased, it was okay for her to be free, and presumably, start over. She acknowledged his death as a doorway out of our over-stressed relationship, but she also admitted that she couldn't understand her own behavior. I think a psychiatrist would have understood it. I sort of understood it—Jewell was ruled by her father.

A divorce is not only between two individuals but also affects family and friends. It took a couple of years for my sorrow to turn into anger. I was angry not just for myself but for all of our extended family. I felt close to Harriet, her mother, and she sent me comforting letters, hoping to stay in touch. But I knew there was no point and had to let her go as well.

I was free now to move into the city and pursue my dream of being an artist. This was something I had always wanted to do but Jewell was not too keen on living in New York. I scraped together what little money I had and moved into a deteriorated brownstone in the DUMBO (Down Under Manhattan Bridge Overpass) section of Brooklyn. I found the place by chance during an artist's studio tour of the neighborhood. Like a lot of old dwellings in New York, it had an aura of decayed elegance—wide floorboards, bricked-up fireplace, heavy French doors that slid into a wall, and a crumbling ceiling wreath for a long-gone chandelier. The rooms were huge, and the long windows barred. Built in Walt Whitman's time, it served as a boarding house for sailors who disembarked a few blocks away at the mouth of the East River. I was very excited to be there, embracing a new life. The rain was incessant on moving day.

AFTERWORD

New York would not have been to Jewell's liking; she was a small-town girl at heart and Port Chester was our compromise. And although my experience in the city would not lead to that youthful dream of being an independent artist, getting paid for what you do like anyone else, at least I can say I had the good struggle and can speak my truth. I didn't want fame, I just wanted to survive; there are plenty of artists in New York who are able to do just that without having to teach. Good luck.

I did, however, have the opportunity to meet and/or work with a few famous artists: Claes Oldenburg, Judy Pfaff, Howard Hodgkin, Al Held, Alex Katz, et al. When I was a student at SUNY Purchase, I was part of a crew that fabricated Oldenburg's "Crusoe Umbrella" for the Castelli Gallery in New York in 1980. It was a life-sized replica of the one located on the Civic Center Plaza in Des Moines, Iowa. This one was made entirely of laminated balsa wood, painted to resemble

230

the original steel sculpture that is fifty-seven feet long and thirty-three feet high. Of course the gallery is not that big, so the replica was made to fit into the room as if it intersected the ceiling and continued through the imagined floors above. The "handle" of the umbrella poured down from the ceiling in the back room. Unless you were looking at the small model on display for context, you wouldn't know what you were looking at since the bottom arc of the umbrella and its handle were quite abstract when viewed in this piecemeal manner. The parts of this puzzle were so large we couldn't get them into the building in the usual way through the alley-side of the gallery, so we took them in through the front. I rode on the flatbed of the truck, standing behind the cab as we drove around to the other side. I felt like Caesar on a chariot, coming to conquer the Gauls; I was so glad to be in New York, and too young to consider failure as any part of my future. It took us twenty-two hours, working straight through the night, to get it up in time for the opening. Afterwards, Mr. Oldenburg took us out for dinner in Chinatown. Having admired the casual draftsmanship of his drawings and washes, I asked him how he liked printmaking, as evidenced in his lithographs. He said he enjoyed etching the most because it was more "sculptural." By saying it was sculptural he was referring to the fact that etching involves the creation of physical reservoirs for the ink on a metal plate as opposed to the planographic chemistry of lithography. I thought that rather strange. Sometimes these blue-chip artists get overloaded by admiring fans and say something silly. Perhaps he simply didn't have a soulful enough connection with whoever his printer was for the lithos. In any event, I found the expressiveness of his lithographs to be closer to my own sensibilities as a painter, and his etchings to be too hard and more inclined towards the conceptual. Later, we bade him a good evening and watched as he walked away into the dark wet streets of Chinatown. He made quite an enigmatic impression: a clear plastic bag slung over his shoulder that held a Mickey Mouse coloring book—perhaps it would serve as inspiration for his next project.

My teachers at Purchase were Scott Richter, Nicholas ("Nick") Marsicano, Margot Lovejoy, and Antonio Frasconi—all nationally, and internationally known, artists. The printmaking teachers encouraged me to show my portfolio to Robert Blackburn at his famous printmaking studio in the city. I think it was Margot who said, "He's very supportive of young printmakers." So I went and showed. His only comment was, "You'll never make it in New York." What generosity! But I did have some exhibitions including a group show at the prestigious Alternative Museum. I was also given a one-person show at the St. Marks Gallery in the East Village, a good place to be in the 1980s. I'm afraid it's true though, for the majority of people, that the only thing you can do with an art degree is teach—having to work full time at anything else is a trap for an artist. I was too penniless and too much in debt to continue towards a master's degree. With superfluous connections, and little support financial or otherwise, New York will eat you alive. I was there for ten years and mugged several times. Blackburn was right.

Gentleman of the Road

When I was in my mid-thirties, my mother and I were able to piece together a relationship. She told me that she had been diagnosed with agoraphobia, which explained a lot of the hysteria and the "craziness" of her personality. I'm sure there was more to her that went undiagnosed—she was also quite codependent—but that was the main problem. She was suffering with this condition for years and it was probably why she left George; she may have been having panic attacks out in the desert—but didn't know why. So she made up stories about being dumped by him because no one, back in the day, would have understood her condition or the cause of these attacks. If anything, they would have blamed her for her marital problems—and she would not have understood her own illness. It was hard not to forgive her after hearing this and I'm sorry it took so long for her to get help. Elroy truly was her protector, or enabler, even though he had no idea what her problem was for all those years. Of course, he made me out to be the villain because I had abandoned them both to live my own life. I was the convenient scapegoat. And so, I escaped, what else are you supposed to do?

I had remarried; another disaster. Many of the women I met, or became involved with, in the city were raging narcissists. My mother was probably the prototype: a narcissist of the "broken wing" variety. I guess we're attracted to what's familiar—even if it's bad.

After two divorces I finally met Cass, my best friend and the love of my life. We've been together now for thirty years and counting. Before our escape from New York, I took apart dozens of my large-scale paintings and discreetly tossed them into unwary dumpsters. Stretcher bars lined the sidewalk free for the taking. These were gone within minutes, devoured by the hungry artists living in nearby lofts in this city of dreams. Despite the difficulties of survival in the Big Apple, and the obvious disappointments, I can't be cynical about it because, after all, that's where I met Cass. And if not for a series of missteps, or even the hostilities engendered by my parents, I never would have ended up in New York, and never experienced anything outside of the Midwest. The world is in flux and everything changes.

Throughout all these early experiences I was glad to have had the *I Ching* as a tool for deciphering the uncharted randomness that life throws at you. My understanding of the *I Ching* concluded with the realization that you probably knew what the path was, you just wanted some confirmation. And choosing the right path often becomes less of an uncertainty as you age. Nevertheless, there is an ambiguity in choice. You may think that you've been presented with many obvious choices, but how did you get there? The possibilities you were contemplating depends on where you were at that moment— arrived at by a series of chance happenings. To misquote Fernando Pessoa (or rather, one of his heteronyms), the future has a thousand possibilities and the past no longer exists, so it's best to stay in the present. To use the *I Ching* is to understand that present moment, and I found it to be very uncanny in its accuracy and directness. I never disagreed with

234

a received hexagram—I simply tried to understand what it was pointing at. If I didn't understand, it was because either the question wasn't clear enough or the hexagram was addressing an underlying thought, or condition of reality, that I wasn't conscious of. I wondered if John Cage used it only for his art or did he use it in his personal life as well? Cage is the only artist I know of whose creations, being outside of personal choice, are in tune with nature. Is art separate from life?

I wondered if the *I Ching* had anything to say about the ending of this book. How should it end? Framing the question in this way is to ask the book of its opinion. After throwing the coins, this is the response: *Hsieh/Deliverance*, which changes to *K'un / The Receptive*. In the primary hexagram, *Hsieh*, we have the removal of obstacles and the resolution of difficulties, but deliverance is not yet obtained. This hexagram represents the stages one must go through to obtain deliverance. It goes on to talk about not going farther than you need, and to bring things back to normal as soon as possible. Further comments in "The Image" section yields this nugget of not dwelling on failings that come to light, like mistakes and unintentional transgressions.

There are plenty of mistakes in my memory of these events. I rely mostly on the bricks of my journal keeping, and the filling in of cracks with whatever daubing my muddied memory brings. Looking back, it's easy to see that we really are all players on life's stage, as the saying goes, and that the world really is theater. But we don't have to believe that our roles are a concrete reality. Life is change, and you're free to move about the cabin.

The second and fourth lines are the ones that change this hexagram to *K'un / The Receptive*. Since these lines change, their particular commentary is heeded. According to Taoist Master Alfred Huang, one needs only to pay attention to the lower changing line. And with that, the oracle reveals an obstruction that must be removed if one is to gain deliverance, or relief, by keeping a straight course through measures adopted as a means for this end. The image of a hunt and of an arrow is presented; the arrow is the straight course. I think this points to the necessity of truthfulness in a memoir; truth being the arrow, the straight course. None of the conversations in this book were verbatim and most were made up for the purpose of moving the story along. But the story, or the essence of it, is nonetheless true.

The second hexagram that *Hsieh* changes into is, as mentioned in an earlier chapter, *K'un*—the receptive. It's the yin in the yin/yang symbol; the receptive, the Earth; devotional and responsive to *Ch'ien*, the creative. The image of a mare is presented, suggesting the tireless roaming of a horse over a great expanse of land (not a bad image for a hitchhiking memoir!). This is the physical aspect of Nature wherein the creative impulse of Spirit can be realized. The symbol of a mare is made specifically to represent receptivity and gentleness. In human terms this refers to someone who does not lead but rather acquiesces to guidance. I would interpret this as an

236

active reflection, an acknowledgement, of the people who have helped me write this memoir. And to those who gave us good rides and safe passage across this "great expanse of land."

AUTHORS NOTE

This is a true story of a hitchhiking adventure with my girlfriend in the 1970s. We traveled across Canada and the United States in search of a place to call home. I relied upon my journal to keep a chronological record of the events and my memory to bring those events to life. Conversations are fabricated, but are not dissimilar to what was said, in order to keep the story, and the spirit of it, moving. While on the road I used the *I Ching*, the Chinese Book of Changes, to determine and interpret the decisive response needed for any obstacle that presented itself. All of the hexagrams obtained, and my response to them, are recorded exactly as they occurred. Most of the names of individuals have been changed to preserve anonymity.

ACKNOWLEDGEMENTS

Writing, like painting, is a solitary act, but like a large sculpture, it takes a team to bring it to life and make it happen. I'm grateful to Abby Macenka at Between the Lines Publishing for understanding the nature of this book, and wish to thank my editors, Deb Alix and Misty Mount, for their insight and suggestions.

I would also like to thank my friend Catherine Madison for her feedback on my first draft and sharing her expertise about writing memoirs.

As always, I'm grateful to my wife, Cass, for her love, support, and input in the creation of this project.

Rollie Erickson is an artist whose paintings have been exhibited nationally and abroad. His work has been reproduced in various catalogs and in *Art in America, 1984–85 Guide to Galleries, Museums, Artists*. He is the founder of *Wordimage*, a single-issue magazine that explored text-imagery as well as contemporary surrealist poetry. In 2017, he published *Night Palaces*, his first book of poetry. His poetry has also appeared in: *Asheville Poetry Review*, *Art/Life*, and *O!! Zone*.

Rollie has a BFA from Purchase College SUNY and an MLIS in library studies from The University of North Carolina Greensboro.

Gentleman of the Road: A Hitchhiking Memoir of the 1970s is his first book of prose.

9 781958 901489